THE BOY IN THE BOX

THE
BOY
IN
THE
BOX

A NOVEL

LEE J. NELSON

BRIDGE WORKS PUBLISHING COMPANY
Bridgehampton, New York

Published by Bridge Works Publishing Company, Bridgehampton, New York, a member of the Rowman & Littlefield Publishing Group.

Distributed in the United States by National Book Network, Lanham, Maryland. For descriptions of this and other Bridge Works books, visit the National Book Network website at www.nbnbooks.com.

FIRST EDITION

The characters and events in this book are fictitious. Any similarity to actual persons, living or dead, is coincidental and not intended by the author.

Library of Congress Cataloging-in-Publication Data
Nelson, Lee J., 1954-
    The boy in the box : a novel / Lee J. Nelson.— 1st ed.
        p. cm.
    ISBN 1-882593-66-9 (alk. paper)
1. Young men—Fiction. 2. Employment interviewing—Fiction. 3. Identity (Psychology)—Fiction. 4. New York (N.Y.)—Fiction. 5. Kidnapping—Fiction. 6. Boys—Fiction. I. Title.
    PS3614.E446 B74 2003
    813'.6—dc21

                                                                2002007276

∞ ™ The paper used in this publication meets the minimum requirements of American National Standard for Information Sciences—Permanence of Paper for Printed Library Materials, ANSI/NISO Z39.48–1992.
Manufactured in the United States of America.

"Such the confusion between real and—how say its
contrary?"

—**Samuel Beckett,** *Ill Seen, Ill Said*

THE
BOY
IN
THE
BOX

ONE

On a hot and humid day in August 1999, Smith dropped off his bags in his sister's Queens, New York, apartment, having just arrived from the West Coast, and was on his way out for something to eat when he came upon the janitor mopping the hallway. In an undershirt, the straps of which hardly constrained his hairy shoulders, the man was backing up, swiveling from side to side, steering the stringy mop. In order to reach the lobby, Smith had to squeeze past the shoulders and the mop and in the process deposited his shoeprints on the washed and gleaming floor.

"Sorry about that," he offered uselessly.

The janitor waved and smiled to show that no offense was taken. He looked at Smith as if the two were old friends though Smith had never before laid eyes on the man. From behind a pair of thick glasses and beneath a corona of black, unruly hair, the janitor gazed without blinking and with an eagerness that Smith found unsettling. The welcome was too warm, Smith thought, too familiar. The eyes were luminous and intelligent, but the jaw and cheeks were knobby and unshaved—a caveman's face, crude but sensitive, and Smith's first acquaintance in his new and interim home.

Also observing him on moving day was the janitor's wife. Her first-floor apartment overlooked the entrance to the building, and Smith saw her seated in the window, leaning out across the sill gazing over a garden where a rosebush was in bloom. She was watching the street, eyeing the passersby. A low brick wall and scrawny hedges enclosed the garden, and, in the ensuing days, Smith would notice neighbors push between the hedges, step to the wall and chat with the janitor's wife. Now, as Smith walked by, wanting to be friendly, he nodded toward the figure in the window, but she stayed rock still; not even her eyes shifted in recognition. Later, he would see her up close, see that she was squat and square, that the long black dress she always wore covered her like a drop cloth, that a tufted mole sat on her jaw like a cactus, that lines of gray knotted her hair and a vague mustache shadowed her lip. Of course, at that first sighting, he had not known that this woman was the janitor's wife, a particular fact he surmised upon returning from the grocery with a dozen eggs and a container of orange juice and finding the happy-eyed janitor himself sitting in the window, smoking a cigarette and smiling at the street.

By the morning of his second day, Smith perceived a pattern: While the other windows of the janitor's apartment were hidden behind venetian blinds, a living body was almost permanently present in that one window overlooking the garden. Nor was the figure simply taking air; it was observing, guarding the entrance, noting who came and who went. In the evening, it was often the janitor, silhouetted darkly against the bluish flicker of a television that was constantly on. In the daytime, it was usually the wife, motionless like a pallid mushroom blending with its circumstances. Occasionally, the teenage son took his turn: a burly boy with a bored, bulldog grimace. A smoker, like his father, he kept a cigarette pack snug in the breast pocket of his tight T-shirt. There were always eyes on duty, Smith realized, always an ugly gargoyle smoking or sunning itself, defending hearth and home.

Burglary was a problem everywhere, and Smith appreciated the added security provided by a family of omniocular gargoyles while neighboring buildings stood unattended. On the other hand, his comings and goings would be witnessed. He planned on taking walks and expected, not infrequently, to step outside, be surprised by the weather and march back in for a change of clothes; or, having visited the grocery and already gone upstairs, to remember a forgotten container of milk and return outside to complete the shopping. And he wondered: Was the gargoyles' purpose to protect the building against intruders or to monitor the tenants, note their habits, their schedules, their visitors? He felt keenly the loss of privacy, and striking him as especially awkward was the obligation, as he came and went, of having to acknowledge in some way the sentinel in the window.

As a response he formulated a policy. Passing through the gargoyles' domain covered four distinct routes: exiting from the building and turning right, to the south; exiting and turning left; approaching and entering from the north; and from the south. Only the second route, he decided, exiting and heading north, passing right by the window, face-to-face as it were, warranted a salutation: a nod, a smile, a wave of the hand. On day two, as he left the building and turned left, he did wave to the son, but the boy reacted disdainfully, sneering and flicking his cigarette ash at Smith's feeble endeavor at communication.

He reconsidered: Perhaps his privacy was not under siege; perhaps the gargoyles shied from his gaze just as he flinched inwardly from theirs.

On moving day, after unpacking his clothes and toiletries and storing, in the hall closet, his suitcases, new suit, and the portfolio containing the sketches of his designs, he had called his sister in Boston, where she was staying until September 1. He was subletting her apartment, and when she returned in two weeks, he would move out and find his own place.

Her phone rang, and the answering machine picked up with a recording of her exuberant voice: "Hi! I'm not home now, but I'd love to talk to you, so leave your name and number, and I'll get back to you as soon as I can. See ya!" The beep followed, and Smith left his message, stating simply that he had arrived, that all had gone well, that he would try reaching her again soon if he did not hear from her first.

The one-bedroom apartment was suitable for his needs. It had a foyer and a narrow hall with the kitchen to the right and the living room, bathroom and bedroom farther back to the left. The living room had wood floors, a comfortable sofa, a floor lamp, a writing desk, and a television. The mattress in the bedroom was firm, but the room was hot and had no air conditioner. On the writing desk were two ballpoint pens, a yellow pad and six books standing up between bookends: two telephone books, a cookbook, a dictionary, a biography of the actress Gloria Stevens and a city guide, inside of which he found a fold-up street map and a map of the subway system. The apartment faced east toward a flattened skyline of residential rooftops, and from the window in his kitchen he could overlook the approach to the building, the rose garden and the roosting gargoyles, though the angle was too sharp to reveal more than a set of forearms or fingers grasping a cigarette.

He had arrived on a Saturday, and the next Thursday he would have a job interview for a position in the Industrial Design Division of the Berenson Corporation, a consumer product manufacturer. In his wallet he carried the company's business card, which had the address of its offices in the Conrad Building in midtown Manhattan. As an applicant, Smith had much to his credit: He was in good health, with a fresh master's degree in industrial design from a prestigious West Coast university. He was personable and confident but not carelessly optimistic about his chances. The possibility of failing did not alarm him. He was determined but not driven. He intended to set up contacts at other companies and businesses, and, in the end, if nothing worthwhile came through, he would go back to the West Coast and establish a life there.

Professionally, while looking forward to producing designs of his own creation, he was also comfortable improving existing products. Yet he possessed a unique and personal thumb, and the prospect of impressing it on the landscape of everyday design inspired him to think creatively. He viewed product development as a series of gradual modifications, many imperceptible to the untrained eye. These modest adjustments influenced everything around them, rippling outward like unseen waves of change. He preferred working on household items and believed with them he would find a niche for himself. He had assembled a portfolio of works-in-progress, which he expected to review before his interview. His most complete sketch was for a polyethylene garbage can lid, which would neither stick nor tear when yanked; a latch pried the top up as the handle was lifted, and the latch itself was detachable and could be washed separately. Another promising idea was for a dustpan that revolved on an axis, not unlike a revolving door.

As a designer, he fit comfortably within the well-known schools. He favored clarity, balance, even tones and basic shapes. He appreciated, for example, the chest of drawers in his sister's bedroom, with its straight edges and lack of trim; the austerity stressed its practicality and presented an unambiguous starting point. He relied on familiar analytical strategies: Separate an object's function from its form, its color from the material, its overall aesthetic impression from its purpose and place in the landscape of utility; then rebalance the elements, creating something new.

When commencing a design, he positioned the project beneath a mental template of geometric figures. Initially he had conceived his revolving dustpan through an image of succeeding right triangles, but as the model turned, the triangular pans failed to mesh, so he broadened the angles and tried more obtuse forms, which produced, after much revision, a hopeful diagram. He believed that even the most unruly of contraptions could be placed in context and thereby become beautiful, functional and cost-efficient. Design disclosed the here and now by constraining the sensory blur—by shaping it and using it—compelling him to connect to his world; no other technology promised to be as effective or as long-lasting.

Aside from street noises and traffic sounds, an occasional dog barking, footfalls from neighbors overhead and intermittent drilling and hammering from the apartment next door, his apartment, 4B, was quiet though oppressively warm. It was located on a long hallway, in a building with seventy-one apartments, and, although he was staying only a short time, he hoped to get to know his neighbors. While chance meetings did occur, the building mostly reverberated with missed encounters. On almost each trip into the hallway, he heard a door slam or glimpsed an indistinct figure slip across a threshold and vanish behind the resounding bolt of locks. Once, as the elevator was in motion, the cables churning, he listened but detected no other noises. Then the elevator was silent, stopped at some other floor. By the time it reached his, the car was empty. He began to feel like a traveler in a budget motel, whose fellow guests stayed to themselves in separate rooms, snugly wrapped in discrete and uniquely complicated lives. This disconnectedness troubled him at first, but, considering the gargoyles, he soon recognized an advantage to the anonymity, which shielded him from the nosiness of strangers.

He did cross paths with a few of his neighbors. On moving day, returning from the grocery, he came upon an old man in the vestibule fumbling with his keys. Smith opened the door for him, and they headed toward the elevator. The man was at least seventy, wearing a tan suit and polished brown shoes, and had difficulty walking; he had to slide his hand along the wall for support and keep an eye on his feet. Two steps led up from the lobby to the hallway where the mailboxes and elevator were situated. Confronting the challenge presented by these steps, the man paused, caught his breath, braced his hand against the wall, lifted his stiff right leg and planted the foot on the lower step, followed it more quickly with the left foot, then paused again before tackling the higher step. When the elevator arrived, Smith opened the door and waited.

"Don't," the man said. "I have to check the mail."

"No problem." Smith held the door.

"No, no, go ahead. You opened one door for me already. That's enough."

"Two's my limit," Smith joked, continuing to wait.

The man opened the dented brass door of the mailbox, removed a letter, closed and locked the mailbox, and, with his head down, trudged into the elevator and pressed the button for the fifth floor. Smith expected a word of thanks, or at least an appreciative glance, but instead the man turned to face the corner, keeping his back toward Smith, not to screen from Smith's prying eyes the contents of the letter, which he clutched with trembling hands and did not open. The man had turned, it seemed, simply to show Smith his back.

At first, Smith was angered by the undeserved snub. Then he speculated: The man might have had a problem with the light; he might have begun weeping or was afraid of catching germs or of spreading germs; perhaps he stood in the elevator that way even when alone and did not consider the posture impolite; or else he was ashamed of his frailty and wobbliness.

A more auspicious exchange had taken place earlier that day soon after his arrival. As he got off the elevator, lugging his bags and portfolio, panting and perspiring, a family approached from down the hall: a girl in a pink dress; a boy with a tie and pomaded hair; a father, stocky, paunchy, balding, with a bulbous nose; and the mother, who came last, having lingered to lock the apartment door. Taller, thinner and younger than her husband, she had long brown hair, a buoyant smile and green eyes that squinted out of cheerfulness. To Smith, at first glance, the two made an incongruous couple. She appeared to be about thirty years old; he was over forty. They introduced themselves: He was Edgar, she was Carin. Edgar remarked how difficult it was moving to a new home. It had taken her over a year to adjust after she had moved in, Carin added, and then she offered assistance: They lived in apartment 4F; if Smith needed anything, he should feel free to ask; if she could help, she would. Smith was grateful but explained that the only task remaining was to unpack and take a shower. The adults laughed. Edgar and Carin spoke with foreign accents, his thick, hers hardly noticeable. The young boy, maybe eight years old, stood in front of his father while the older man's husky hands gripped his son's shoulders. The boy's clean and curious face looked up at Smith. The shy and impatient girl, older than her brother, went inside the elevator, where her parents and brother joined her. As if seeing the family off on a voyage, Smith waved through the small porthole window in the elevator door and kept waving even as the cables groaned and started lowering the car.

That first evening he stayed in and watched television. It was extremely hot and sticky, and to stay cool he moved as little as possible. He skimmed channels with the remote control, flicking through comedies and celebrity interviews, glancing at a movie called *Deeper Suspicion,* a thriller about a housewife terrorized by her husband. He settled on another movie called *The Chameleon,* a romance about a wry, sophisticated ne'er-do-well who convinced perfect strangers to adore him but was seen for what he really was by only one, the object of his spurned affections, the beautiful daughter of a wealthy businessman. Smith was impressed by how the urbane con artist charmed and flirted in hotel lobbies, in train stations, at cocktail parties, always making clever and alluring remarks. As the plot unfolded, it became less convincing, cluttered with improbable coincidences, a noisy car chase, and finally an unlikely murder of which the Chameleon was falsely suspected.

He never learned the Chameleon's fate. He had assumed the man would be cleared of the murder charge, reform his behavior and marry the beautiful woman, but as the film entered its final quarter hour, Smith's door was assaulted by three pounding knocks.

He leaped up. Who could be visiting at that hour?

He shut off the television. A few seconds passed, then a heavy thud sounded from the hallway. Smith peeked through the peephole, saw no one, opened the door and spotted, at the end of the hall, the janitor kneeling by the closet reserved for discarded newspapers and recyclables. The man had on the same white undershirt he had been wearing earlier, but, rather than a mop, he was wielding a box cutter and bundling newspapers with string.

He stopped work and smiled as Smith approached.

"Excuse me. Did someone just knock on my door?"

The man stood up, adjusted his glasses and muttered gruffly and unintelligibly in a heavily accented and smoke-clogged voice.

"Excuse me?"

The janitor repeated the indistinct phrase, which sounded to Smith's ear like "abastaboy" and, judging by the pleased look on the man's face, referred to something he enjoyed.

"I'm having difficulty understanding you," Smith said.

He smelled alcohol and sweat, and as the janitor reached up toward him, he jerked back, but the man had no intention of touching him; instead, he ran his open hands up and down in front of Smith as if stroking him through the air but making no contact. His eyes gleamed with that presumptuous familiarity that Smith had found so disquieting earlier.

Smith took another step back.

"Smoove," the janitor mumbled. He steered his palm and fingers in front of Smith's face, tracing in air the physiognomy, running his illusory touch along the shape of Smith's forehead, down his cheek, cupping his chin. "Butiful!" He breathed heavily through his mouth. "Like abasta."

"Abasta?"

"Smoove." He glided his hand over an unseen surface, denoting smoothness. "Abasta."

"Alabaster?"

The janitor shook his head to affirm that Smith had guessed right though Smith had no idea what was meant.

"Abasta boy!"

"Alabaster boy?"

"Yes!" the janitor crooned exultingly.

"Who is alabaster boy?"

The man looked down the hallway and up the staircase to make sure no one else was listening. "You," he whispered, giggling. He then sighed, closed his eyes and crossed his hands over his chest, as if seized by a tender feeling. The sallow hallway, feebly lit by circular fluorescent bulbs, framed the grotesque icon.

Smith was alarmed. "I'm sorry, but you're obviously mistaking me for someone else. We've never met before."

The janitor shook his finger, then pointed to his head. "I know you," he declared, leering intrusively.

"Excuse me, sir, but I am certain we have never met before. Would you mind telling me where and when?"

"Shhh!" The janitor cautioned silence, then launched a narration that was virtually incomprehensible, punctuated by throaty growls, ventings of pleasure, arm waves, whorls, figure eights, and one solid firming of his hands by his chest as if he were holding a melon. He smiled throughout. His teeth were brown from neglect, and his hair, growing uncombed in all directions, was like a forest of black, tousled trees.

Smith interrupted, annoyed by the presumption that he should make sense of the man's incoherence. "Could you please repeat what you just said. I did not understand you."

"Shhh!" Again the gargoyle urged quiet, raising a finger to his mouth to preempt all objections. He stopped smiling and adopted a serious expression, preparing to disclose a matter of importance. To indicate "Listen!" he tapped his ear, then took a step toward Smith, who held his ground. He looked at the stairwell, then down the hall. Finding they were alone, he said: "Boyd'bok."

"Excuse me?"

"Boy." He gestured with his palms toward his knees. "Bok." His fingers shaped a rectangle in the air.

Smith shook his head. "I don't understand."

The janitor frowned, wrestling with his broken words. He pointed at Smith. "Boy."

"Boy?"

The janitor nodded vigorously. With his hands he indicated that something was inside something else and with his index fingers again traced in air the shape of a rectangle: "Bok."

Smith sighed, fully perplexed.

The janitor looked around and from the recycling closet pulled out a small cardboard box, declaring: "Bok!"

"A box?"

"Yes! Boy inside."

"A boy inside a box?"

"Yes!"

"You're telling me there's a boy inside a box."

"Yes!" Having finally made himself understood, he glowed from the triumph and the relief.

"A cardboard box?"

"No." The janitor shook his head. "Wut."

"A wood box?"

"Yes!"

"A box made out of wood."

"Yes!"

"A wooden box with a boy inside."

"Yes! Yes! Naket boy!" His eyes flashed.

"A naked boy in a wooden box?"

"Naket boy!" The janitor seemed stirred by his enunciation of the phrase, which, compared to the rest of his vocabulary, was fairly well articulated.

Smith realized he could be talking to a madman, that he should have excused himself right away. He had come out only to discover who had knocked on his door, and the janitor obviously had mistaken him for somebody else. But he was unsure of how much validity the man's tale might have.

"Where is this box?" Smith asked.

"Outside."

"Where outside?"

The janitor shrugged. He did not know.

"Who knows?" Smith asked, showing frustration.

The janitor proceeded to mime a beggar, proffering his palm and uttering plaintive pleas. From arduous verbal exchanges and decoding, Smith gleaned that the character being portrayed was called a "true beggar" or "one true beggar" who knew of, had heard of, had possession of or was interested in selling a wooden box in which a naked boy was being held, presumably against his will. Whether this boy was alive or dead, a real boy or an imaginary boy; whether the box was real or invented; whether the man had meant "peddler" instead of "beggar," Smith failed to determine from the presentation, which was rushed, secretive and generally impossible to understand. At one point a woman emerged from the elevator and glanced suspiciously at the two men, compelling the janitor to drop onto one knee and start busying himself with the newspapers. His testimony resumed only after the woman entered her apartment and the hallway stopped rumbling from the closing of her door. He then mentioned Chinatown though in what context remained unclear. Overall, the janitor talked about the boy with a deep seriousness and sense of urgency and left Smith with the unlikely impression that only he, Smith, would be able to locate and rescue this boy. Again, the man spoke so confusedly that, in the middle of the narration, Smith asked himself how anyone who had spent any time at all in an English-speaking country could use the language so poorly.

The janitor clasped his hands and pleaded with Smith to find this boy in the box, then dropped again to his knees.

Smith turned and looked down the hall. At the opposite end stood the frumpish wife who had climbed the stairs to the fourth-floor landing and stationed herself by the stairwell. A silent block in her heavy black dress, her arms folded across her mammoth bosom, she watched while the husband, bowed and penitent, as if caught in a misdeed, lugged two bundles of newspapers toward her shrouded bulk, stepped past her without peeking up and started down the stairs. She followed, glancing back vacuously at Smith before descending out of sight.

Smith returned to his apartment preoccupied by the puzzling conversation. Of the confidential information the janitor had struggled to impart, Smith had grasped only a few phrases and even those he was not confident of having understood. He had not learned the man's name, had not wanted to know it, repulsed as he had been by the figure and the gestures and the frothy babble, and by the intimate gleam in the man's eyes, a lambency that had signaled the rewarming of an old acquaintanceship although Smith was certain the two had never seen each other prior to their earlier encounter. Smith shivered, recalling how the man had run his hands in the air as if caressing him, and he leaped up and hurried to make sure that he had bolted the locks on the door.

He returned to the television in time to watch the ten o'clock news, which focused on local stories: a tenement fire, a jewelry store robbery, a serial rapist preying on elderly women. When the photograph of a young boy's smiling face appeared over the shoulder of the anchorwoman, Smith listened attentively: "Billy Sanderson, four years old, disappeared yesterday morning from outside his home in Bayside, Queens. A police task force has been set up to locate the missing boy." On the screen came the boy's uncle, labeled as the family spokesperson, who pleaded for help. There was a picture of the boy's home: a wooden frame house with a lawn, a street where worried neighbors gathered and consoled one another. The anchorwoman concluded: "Billy was last seen wearing a baseball cap, a blue T-shirt, blue jeans and sneakers. Anyone having information regarding his whereabouts is asked to call . . ." Smith jumped up and grabbed the yellow pad and a ballpoint pen, but the number was not repeated; the report was over, replaced by a commercial for a Caribbean cruise.

While the child abduction story fit neatly into the catalogue of broadcast tragedies, it also touched Smith personally. He sensed a slight panic in his stomach and the growing weight of responsibility. His mind contrived an image, a fiction anchored by a hideous fact: a missing boy—Billy Sanderson or another missing boy—trapped and frightened, taken to a secret place, stripped and beaten, his arms and legs bound and crammed, packed inside a wooden box.

The news ended and a talk show began. Smith turned off the sound and gazed with disinterest at the voicelessly chattering, pixelized faces. Drained from the heat, he watched lethargically until he heard quarreling coming from the street. Looking out the kitchen window, he saw, in front of the building, a police car double-parked, its flashing beacons rotating on the roof. A radio crackled. The gargoyles had assembled on the sidewalk; the son's hands were plunged into his pockets, his shoulders slumped; the mother was stationary and acquiescent. They watched as the husband and father, still in his undershirt, his wrists handcuffed behind his back, was gently guided by a policeman into the backseat of the patrol car.

Mother and son waited for the car to drive off, then re-entered the building.

The sky was overcast. There was no other traffic. As far as Smith could discern, no one else had witnessed the incident.

He wondered of what crime the janitor had been accused. He was obviously an immigrant; might he have entered the country illegally? Or was his arrest related in some way to the Sanderson boy who had been stolen from in front of his own home, snatched without a trace?

Smith shut off the television and called his sister. She was still not home. The recording was the same, and at the beep, he repeated his message requesting that she contact him, tightening his voice as he added the words, "please, as soon as you can."

TWO

Smith had trouble sleeping. The steamy August heat kept him tossing and turning, and even with the covers off, his skin was clammy and tingly. Throughout the night he felt insects, mostly imagined, scurrying over him, and what sleep he did get was consumed by a dream. In it, he found himself in a neighborhood he thought to be Chinatown although nothing about the area was particularly Chinese. He saw trash and broken glass and weeds sprouting through cracks in the sidewalk. Darkly framed in an alleyway between two tenements, a peddler was beckoning toward him. His shape was part of the shadows, and while Smith did not recognize him, he sensed that he had seen him before. The man was selling a wooden crate, the kind in which fruits or vegetables were packed and shipped. Smiling, he displayed his merchandise; one of the wooden slats had a metal handle, and it opened like a little door.

Inside was squeezed a live naked boy: His legs were folded to his chest, and his head was tilted, his whole body constricted; his nose was caked with blood; his eyes were puffy, black and blue, half-closed, and his swollen, encrusted mouth gulped air like a fish.

In addition to the nightmare, drilling and hammering from the apartment next door awakened Smith at one in the morning, and the racket continued sporadically until five. If the noise returned the next evening, he would have to talk to the neighbor, and if he did not receive satisfaction, he would go to the superintendent.

For breakfast, he ate two boiled eggs and afterward lounged on the sofa, watching the sun slant across the floorboards and touch the opposite wall. He intended to begin that morning preparing for his interview, jotting down questions he would probably be asked and composing answers, which he then could revise and rehearse. He also needed to review his drawings; the curvature of the dustpan lip could be refined, and he considered subduing the scallop motif on the garbage can lid.

As he got up to get the portfolio out of the closet, he heard a woman's voice coming from the street. He went into the kitchen and looked out the window. Carin, his neighbor from 4F, was down by the rose garden speaking a foreign language to the janitor's wife who was perched in her first-floor window. Carin had pushed between the shrubs and stepped up to the low brick wall to stand nearer the building and be heard more easily. She was wearing a white blouse, which gleamed in the sunshine, forming a cheerful, slender image. Smith, in his mind, had difficulty placing her alongside the bald and stocky husband. As he watched, Carin did all the talking while the female gargoyle listened with her forearms folded, hushed and knowing like a sphinx.

Looking out the window, he became restless and realized that he could not spend his first full morning in New York City sitting at a desk, so he put on his shoes, combed his hair, grabbed his wallet and keys and headed out to explore.

He was still puzzled by his discussion with the janitor the evening before. Among the more unsettling particulars were the scene with the police and the man's insistence that he and Smith had known each other. Smith's sister, before she left, may have mentioned his planned arrival to the building superintendent, but he saw no reason why she would have spoken about him to the janitor. "Smith" was not even listed on the intercom directory downstairs, his sister having removed the nameplate, presumably for reasons of security. In the vestibule, on his way out, he paused to scan that directory. Other tenants had similarly opted for anonymity and removed their names, but among the apartments with names still attached he found 1G, which he determined to be the gargoyles' lair. The name listed there was "Dezmun."

By the time he stepped outside, both Carin and the female Dezmun were gone. Stationed in the window was the son. Smith lifted his hand to wave hello, and that was when the boy, in reply, flicked his smirk and cigarette. Smith slunk away and formulated, then and there, his gargoyle-greetings policy.

It would be another hot and hazy day. On the news the night before the weather report announced that the summer had been hotter than most and that the sultry temperatures would continue for at least a few more days. Smith intended to explore close to home. The streets of the neighborhood ran north to south: quiet, tree-lined, residential troughs. Few buildings stood higher than three or four stories, and many of the houses sported lively flower gardens. Avenues ran east to west and bustled commercially. He passed a bakery, a vegetable market, a fish market, a butcher shop with skinned rabbits hanging from hooks in the window. A discount store had spilled its wares onto the sidewalk: paper towels, toilet paper, aluminum foil, towel racks, bedroom slippers, soap dishes. Smith noted the transparent design and cheap materials. He lifted the lid off a steel trash can that was being sold for $22.99. The lid was heavy and did not fit properly on the can; trying to replace it made him feel clumsy. Though his own polyethylene lid had not yet been perfected, clearly it would be superior.

There was much to examine, and he was full of ideas.

He entered a supermarket and roamed the aisles of food and household goods: from bags of beans and lentils to liquid soap, from chocolate bars to can openers, from yeast and spices to packages of instant soup. The fresh produce aisle was the brightest, with apricots and nectarines piled in dewy pyramids. The meat and dairy aisle was the widest: milk, yogurt, cheese, eggs refrigerated on one side; on the other, red meats glistening under cellophane packaging. Softly bathed in background music, shoppers steered metal carts, many of which were laden with what might have been hundreds of dollars of merchandise, mountains of goods that were halted every few feet as the shoppers acquired more products from the shelves. Smith paused among the household cleansers, inspected the dustpans and the brooms. The dustpans in particular made him smile: variations of a single theme; hard rubber or plastic, flat pans, sloping lips, steep walls, oblong handles with hang holes. He marveled at how his revolving dustpan would stand out among this pedestrian collection. After twenty minutes, having wandered up and down all nine aisles, he exited through the electronic doors, not having purchased a single item.

As he passed a bagel shop, a poster in the window caught his eye. It introduced an organization, "Find The Children," and showed the picture of a handsome boy named Timothy Brown, aged four. Beneath the photo were listed his height, weight, hair, eye color; the date, time and place he had last been seen; an appeal for information. Without a pen or pencil to write down the toll-free telephone number, he would have to return later to copy it down.

Smith bought a newspaper and stopped for lunch at a coffee shop. The booths had wooden trim and vinyl seats, and he selected one along the wall. A busboy in a black vest and bow tie cleared the table. His brown cheeks were scarred and pitted, but his hands were deft and delicate as they set the tabletop with a napkin, knife and fork, a menu and ice water in a plastic glass. In other booths, men in suits were eating sandwiches, a white-haired woman was drinking coffee, a mother spooned applesauce into a baby's mouth. At the counter a heavy man whose broad bottom swamped the stool chatted with the cashier while a waitress refilled coffee creamers. The man had a flaccid, jowly face, and his hands were mottled with liver spots. Behind the counter, on the wall, stretched above a long mirror, was a painted frieze of blue-green islands, seabirds and sailboats suspended on an emerald ocean.

"How're you doing?" a waitress asked perkily. She had chestnut hair and brown eyes.

"I'm doing fine," Smith replied. "Just hungry."

"Let's do something about that." She took a pad and pencil out of her apron and smiled, flashing a big overbite, which was quickly reined in by her upper lip.

"What do you recommend?" Smith asked.

She pondered the question and then her eyes widened: "Roast chicken! You can peel off the skin if you'd like."

"Why would I do that?"

"Less fat." She narrowed her eyes and pointed her pencil at Smith as if challenging him. "I bet I know your sign."

"My sign?"

"Your zodiac sign." She nodded knowingly. "You're a Pisces, aren't you?"

"I don't believe I am."

"When's your birthday?"

Smith glanced furtively over his shoulder at the empty booth next to his. "I can't divulge that information," he joked, lowering his voice. "It's a government secret."

"Oh, really!" The waitress laughed. "You are a Pisces. I can tell."

"How do you know?"

"Pisces leave clues."

Smith checked the front of his shirt to see what clues were showing.

Now the waitress lowered her voice: "We Aries have a sixth sense that detects Pisces." She winked, as if it were all a game and she were inviting him to play—telling him also that she was not busy, the lunchtime rush had ended. So much in the blink of an eye!

"And this special sense is a reward for your having been born on a certain date?"

"Nothing happens by coincidence," she stated. "I'm not an Aries because I was born on my birthday. I was born on my birthday because I'm an Aries."

He asked what, if not a birth date, made an Aries an Aries.

"Let's see . . ." She glanced at the ceiling. "What makes a ram a ram?" She tapped the pencil against her chin. "Aries are risk takers. They're pioneers. They're not timid, and they don't necessarily follow the rules."

"But you're not an Aries because you're a risk taker. You're a risk taker because you're an Aries."

"Exactly."

"Actually, I've considered changing my sign."

"You can't do that," she protested.

"Why not? I've been thinking of changing my name, too."

She laughed. Her big smile was all teeth. Smith liked her wit and nonchalance and asked her name, which was Wendy.

The men in suits had finished their sandwiches, and one gestured for the check. The fat man at the counter also turned toward the waitress.

"Got to go," Wendy snapped, all business. "What'll you have?"

"Roast chicken."

"Vegetable: peas, corn, carrots, string beans."

"String beans."

"Potato: fried, mashed, baked."

"Mashed."

"I thought so. Anything to drink?"

"You decide. What would a Pisces drink with his chicken?"

Wendy nodded in sympathy and jotted the answer on the pad. Next, she hurried to the kitchen, shouted Smith's order to the chef, picked up hot plates and hustled among the tables distributing the dishes, giving the men their checks, grinning at their comments, letting drop her own good-natured remarks. Smith enjoyed her breeziness and jaunty style, her sexy overbite, realizing, at the same time, that affability coming from a waitress was often a tool to stir up tips.

As she raced to the kitchen with an overheated face, a curl of hair came loose, and as she tucked it behind her ear, Smith recognized, in that unconscious gesture, an event no astrologer could have predicted.

More diners came in. At the counter, no one sat next to the fat man, whose pants had slipped an inch from his hips, revealing the band of his underwear. He was loud and barked at the cashier, who listened impassively from behind a walrus mustache. Smith skimmed the newspaper. The front page showed a photograph of a man in handcuffs, a doctor who had been arrested for poisoning his patients. Neighbors and friends expressed "shock and disbelief" and described the doctor as "highly respected," a "loving husband," a "wonderful father." Inside were reports on the stock market, a drought in California, a hurricane in Florida. One ghastly crime caught his attention: "Year-Old Tot Tortured." But this child had not been abducted; he had been abused in his own home by his own mother who burned him with cigarettes and forced him into a bathtub of scalding water.

When Smith's food arrived, it immediately disappointed. The chicken was greasy, the string beans overcooked, the potatoes watery and tasting like milk. Smith made a mental note: no more chicken. The only item that pleased him was the cranberry cocktail served in a tall, fluted glass.

As he ate, he leafed through the paper, wading past pages of advertisements, classifieds, gossip columns, sports scores, stock market listings. He found no reference to the missing Sanderson boy or to any other missing child. He paused to check the horoscope and read the entry for Pisces: "This week will be exciting. A career challenge will make your life unpredictable, but use this instability as a source of inspiration. You are not as rigid as others believe. Find your place. Follow your sense of direction." He next read the entry for Aries: "Speak your mind, but don't ignore your doubts. Invite someone to share a new experience. There are always two sides. Face that fact, and you will accomplish much."

The lunch crowd had thinned out.

"Enjoy the drink?" Wendy asked.

"It was perfect."

"Anything else?"

Smith declined, and Wendy totaled up the bill.

"I've been checking up on you," he said, indicating the horoscope. "It suggests here Aries may not be as confident as they appear."

"Oh, really!" She tore the check from the pad and slapped it, face down, on the table. "You look like someone famous," she said, studying Smith with her thoughtful expression until her eyes lit up and the bucktoothed smile emerged. "I know who you look like!" she announced. "Hamilton Baker!"

"Who's he?"

"The actor! You look just like him."

"I don't believe I've ever seen him."

"Oh, you must have." She was incredulous. "I suspect someone's pulling my leg." She winked again, more obviously this time, and was off to greet new customers.

After lunch, Smith continued window-shopping. The humidity had climbed, and his damp shirt clung to his sticky flesh. He bought an ice cream cone and discovered a playground where he sat in the shade on a bench and watched the children. They played soccer and tag, and their steady squeals and shouts collided with the clamor of traffic. A herd of them wore yellow T-shirts showing which daycamp they attended. Counselors strolled among them, trying to control them and be heard. On the bench next to Smith an old man was napping, and farther down, women with head scarves and baby carriages cared for their toddlers. On the benches near the street lived the homeless and the alcoholics, one of whom was just waking up.

Smith thought about the waitress, Wendy, and about his neighbors, Carin and Edgar. Carin was slender and gracious but married to a stumpy leprechaun. Was she really as happy as her beaming face implied? On the other hand, Edgar was friendly, too, and it was very possible, he realized, that the two fit together quite snugly, however discrepant they appeared superficially. Either way, he was pleased that, after only one day, he had met people whom he enjoyed talking to and would likely meet again.

The sky was turning grayer, threatening an afternoon thunderstorm. The counselors had rounded up the campers, who were standing in one crooked line. Smith finished his ice cream, tossed the newspaper into a trash barrel and started back to the apartment. As he headed up the street, he spotted the janitor emerging from an alleyway adjacent to the building. Apparently the man, whom he now knew as Dezmun, had been released from police custody. He had on a red and black striped polo shirt and was wheeling a hand truck to which was strapped an armchair destined for the trash. He unloaded the tattered chair, set it on the curb beside the jumbo bags of garbage, then rolled the hand truck back into the alley, down which Smith peered as he passed, detecting no one. Acknowledging his policy on gargoyle greetings, he tried ignoring the window but was unable to resist glancing once to determine that it was the mother in place, forearms folded like a double windowsill, staring at nothing yet seeing it all.

In the lobby, as he waited by the elevator, a movement at the end of the hall caught his attention. The janitor was standing on the stairs, on the steps halfway down to the basement. With just his upper body visible through the balusters, he resembled a prisoner or an ape in the zoo and was waving at Smith, not making a sound. When the elevator arrived and Smith reached for the door, the janitor's urging grew more frantic.

Smith hesitated. Had the suspect been dangerous, the police probably would not have released him so quickly. He decided to hear what the man had to say before passing judgment.

As he came closer, the janitor headed farther down the stairs toward the poorly lit and deserted basement corridor.

Smith stayed on the landing, growing nervous. "I'm not going down there. If you want to tell me something, you're going to have to tell me here."

Grasping that Smith would not descend with him, the gargoyle conceded and came up a few steps closer to Smith but was still hidden from anyone entering the lobby.

"What's your name?" Smith asked.

"Shhh!"

Smith lowered his voice and spoke slowly and clearly. "My name is Smith. What is your name? Is it Dezmun?"

"Kogat," came the answer.

"Ko-Gat?"

"Kogat."

"Kogat Dezmun?"

The janitor nodded. "I know you," he said.

"That's not possible."

"I know you," he repeated, and his hands started up as if to reach and touch, then dropped to his sides. Smith was alarmed but did not retreat.

What proceeded from Kogat Dezmun, accompanied by apprehensive peeks through the balusters and guided by the ever useful hand gestures, was another turbulent account tangled in a thicket of incomprehensible language. Smith recognized a now familiar description of the boy in the box, who was in some way connected to the one true beggar. Dezmun mentioned Chinatown again, and he repeated pressingly that only Smith could succeed, but at what was unclear; finding the boy, Smith assumed. As sordid and as unintelligible as the man's tale was his manner: leering while describing the most horrible events; staring at Smith without blinking, adjusting his glasses to stare more intrusively; babbling on with the misplaced confidence that Smith was following every word.

Smith cut short the exposition. "If you know anything about a missing boy, you must notify the police."

"No," Dezmun pleaded anxiously.

"Why did the police take you into custody last night?"

"No police," Dezmun insisted. His smile was gone. "No police." He pressed his index finger to his lips.

"Did they ask you about the missing boy?"

He shook his head. "I know noting."

"Who knows?"

"Outside."

Smith was frustrated. "Outside where? Who's outside? The boy?"

Before Dezman could attempt a fuller explanation, the sound of someone entering the lobby sent him scurrying down into the basement. This abrupt retreat made Smith feel guilty as well, and rather than return to the elevator and meet whoever had come into the building, he darted up the stairs, pausing at the second floor to listen to the sounds of the person coughing and opening a mailbox.

Overhead, a boy was looking down from the fourth-floor landing. It was Carin's son, the boy with the pomaded hair and the curious face, which now was riveted on Smith as he came marching upstairs. Smith said hello, asked if the boy's mother and father were at home, asked if the boy was waiting for friends, if he was going to play outside, if he was going to go to the playground. To the first question the boy answered with a simple yes; to the others, a simple no; and between each question he stood silently as Smith grinned. Smith did not begrudge the boy his reticence; while the two had met the day before and technically were no longer strangers, Smith remained sufficiently unfamiliar to warrant discretion. The shy boy gazed at Smith openly and transparently, hiding nothing yet divulging no suggestion of his thoughts.

THREE

Unrelieved by the rainstorm, which never arrived, the moist air by evening had grown steamier. Smith decided if the weather pattern did not change soon, he would purchase an air conditioner.

He sat at the desk in the living room and tried to prepare for his upcoming interview. He straightened the yellow pad and rolled the ballpoint pen between his fingers, finding a comfortable grip. Then, using the binding of the dictionary as a straightedge, he drew a line down the middle of the page. Above the left column he wrote "Questions"; above the right column, "Answers."

That seemed the correct approach, but on which areas should he concentrate? He knew the technical issues and the schools of theory. If presented during the interview with substantive questions that he could not handle, he would admit his ignorance and steer the dialogue back onto familiar paths. He would review his portfolio, of course. Yet he felt the greater need to focus on issues of character and temperament, for the interviewer would want to learn not only the extent and depth of Smith's knowledge and talent but also who Smith was, his family, his friends, his expectations, features that could, more than other elements, shape the applicant as a designer and an employee. First impressions were decisive, and in a terribly short time, perhaps less than five minutes, he needed to present a credible and likable personality.

In the left-hand column, he wrote the broadest of questions: "How would you describe yourself?"

The question sounded flat to him, but he was pleased for having produced it so quickly. He could provide the predictable biographical data, but he wondered whether a more creative response was expected. Unfortunately, he could not picture his interlocutor or understand his or her frame of mind, since he did not even know whether the individual, a Dr. Weber, was a man or a woman.

He tried envisioning the environment. He imagined a crowded antechamber with employees and other visitors, but the interview itself would take place in a quiet office. Pictures would hang on the walls, but styles changed with each reconception: abstracts, landscapes, modernist photographs. He wondered about carpets versus parquet floors, and he predicted he would look out the window and see the river or the skyline.

He put down a second question: "How would you contribute to the firm?" "To begin with," he wrote in the answer column, "I am a person who expects to continue learning throughout his working career." The words were forced. Why did he use the third person? He rephrased: "I intend to continue learning throughout my working career." That was better but equally unsatisfying. It did not answer the question. Why would any firm hire a young man in need of continuous education? He crossed out the sentence and added: "I believe I am a creative person who could bring fresh perspectives to existing problems." He reread the statement and made changes: "I am a creative individual who knows how to use fresh ideas to solve potential as well as existing problems." That was more affirmative but still too stilted and abstract.

He tried a third question: "How do you find working with other people?" Again, he was stumped. His immediate answers were too pedestrian, his subsequent thoughts too detached and technical, others too flip. He was bored by his own platitudes, crossed them out and went on to question four: "What experience have you had in the field of industrial design?" This was the easy question, the one he was hoping to hear, for it would allow him to unzip his portfolio and explicate his work. He tried question five: "What leadership qualities do you possess?" Here, he did not attempt to respond. As far as he could determine, he possessed no leadership qualities and could not even explain what leadership qualities were.

Question number six was interesting: "Why do you want to become an industrial designer?" Answers veered in two directions. He could reply idealistically, exalt the inspiration of his art, the pleasures he received from working creatively while simultaneously improving everyday lives. Or he could describe the opportunities offered by a position in a prestigious company like the Berenson Corporation and how, following years of hard work, he hoped to enter the ranks of management. The first response sounded naive, the second calculating, and the two combined made him appear divided or unable to make up his mind.

He put down his pen and wiped the back of his neck. It was so uncomfortably hot. The apartment's open windows failed to usher in even the hint of a cooling breeze. He gazed at the wall searching for a better strategy and found one: Instead of advancing generalities or clichés, he would tell stories about himself, relate anecdotes: amusing episodes that dramatized his skill, sense of humor, creativity, knowledge, social adeptness—episodes from life that showed him functioning, in context, and speaking for himself, making his real way through the real world. He pictured Dr. Weber, for the moment an older, rigid, dignified gentleman, ensconced behind a mahogany or rosewood desk and swiveling self-confidently in a high-backed leather chair. This applicant was a real person, Dr. Weber would conclude, with concrete experiences more telling and more authentic than data printed on a résumé.

But how was Smith to work these anecdotes into the interview? And where was he to find them? The first episode that came to mind was the incident with the unsteady neighbor who had turned his back on Smith in the elevator; the second involved his interaction with the janitor, Kogat Dezmun. He could hardly kick off the interview, all smiles and handshakes, by mentioning a rude old man or a kidnapped boy. Were Smith to relate either of these experiences, the only reactions he placed on the face of Dr. Weber, male or female, were puzzlement, uneasiness and a firming realization that the current applicant before him or her was not the right man for the job.

Before going to bed, Smith watched a murder mystery on television, much of which consisted of two detectives, a man and a woman, close up in dark scenes, somber and tense, confronting the case at hand: a headless male corpse discovered on the grounds of a girls' boarding school. The detectives conversed in lowered voices, mostly at night, in hallways, in cars, muttering so softly that Smith hardly heard what was said. During a commercial, he called his sister again, left a more terse message on the answering machine—"Call me as soon as you can"—and provided the phone number in case she had forgotten it even though it was her own.

He changed channels at ten o'clock to watch a news broadcast. The top stories included a homeless man set on fire and a foreign tourist shot; coming up were a parade for crippled children, a circus newly arrived in town and a special report on combating odors in the refrigerator. There was nothing about the missing Sanderson boy, nothing about a boy in a box.

A heavy knock at the door jolted him to his feet. His first thought was of the janitor, and his stomach tensed at the prospect of another useless exchange. But when he peered through the peephole, he saw not the older but the younger gargoyle, Kogat Dezmun's son.

Anxiously, Smith opened up.

The young man was not as tall as Smith but was heavier and solid, packed into the T-shirt, his thick arms crossed on his broad chest. He had beady eyes and a baby's face soured to look tough with wide, upturned, piglet nostrils flaring like shotgun barrels.

"Leave the old man alone," he barked, dispensing with introductions. "He didn't bother you, so you got no business bothering him."

Smith was shocked by the tone and suggestion. "I'm not bothering anybody," he protested. "If anybody's being bothered, it's me."

"Cut the crap. Stay away from him. Don't say one word to him."

"Excuse me, but your father came to me and initiated conversation."

"Hey! Don't twist things. Just mind your business. You got a problem with that?"

"Fine."

"You got a problem with that?"

"No, I don't, but let me reiterate: I was minding my business. Your father attracted my attention. He began accosting me with strange stories."

"Hey!" The boy was riled. "Don't you go making charges! Strange stories! My ass!"

To Smith it seemed that no act of reason could resolve the argument.

"You asked him questions," the boy asserted. "How can you be minding your business if you're asking him questions?"

"I had to try to understand what he was saying."

"Why?"

"Why?" Smith suspected a joke, but there was no smile on the boy's mean face. "Why do I try to understand what a person is trying to tell me? Because that's what people do when they are being addressed."

"Where did you come up with that crap?"

The retort's belligerence and lack of logic left Smith bewildered and fatigued. He was dealing with an individual who had difficulty using ideas. He replied as if explaining to a child: "Another person approaches me and speaks to me. I try to understand what it is he is saying. It is called being polite, being civil. It is called behaving properly. Nobody told me about it. I came upon the idea independently. Maybe you should try it."

The boy seethed in silence. Smith feared his sarcasm might have stabbed too sharply, provoking from the steaming hog an angry snort and charge. The youth was breathing hard, with his teeth clenched and his arms wrapped more tightly on his chest.

Instead of blowing up, he spoke calmly: "You talked to him. You asked him questions. That don't sound to me like minding your own business. If you say otherwise, you're a liar."

Now Smith became indignant. "Wait just a minute! I am not a liar, and you have no right to say I am. Your father said something to me that could have involved a missing child. Now if he says something to me about a kidnapped boy in a small wooden box, I'm probably going to listen and most likely ask questions. If in fact he knows something about a missing child, he shouldn't be telling me about it in the first place. He should be telling the police."

At this the son exploded. "You leave those scumbags out of this!" he shouted, unwrapping his arms and making fists, jutting his chin at the air in front of Smith's nose. "First thing an asshole like you does when you can't face up to the truth is call the cops. They got no play here. Unless you're a cop? Are you a cop?"

Fearing that the confrontation could get out of hand and worried that the neighbors might be listening, Smith lowered his voice and tried conciliation. "Listen."

"Are you a cop?"

"I don't want any trouble."

"Answer me. Are you a cop?"

"No, I am not a cop. I just moved in here. I don't know anybody. I'm staying only until the end of this month. With your father, I was just trying to be polite. If you'd rather I didn't talk to him, I'll try not to. I just think it's reasonable to expect equal cooperation from him and unreasonable to assume I will ignore someone who's addressing me, even if it is in some mixed-up language I can't understand, and especially if it might concern the fate of a missing child."

The son glared, but Smith saw that there would not be violence. There was too much flab and bluff in the pink face, and the menacing stare contained a deeper thought, although one too far down for either him or Smith to extract.

Somewhere upstairs, a door opened and closed. The boy smirked and pronounced judgment: "I hate punks like you. I hate you educated shits. You think you're so smart. You're a punk. An educated, big-word piece of crap. I hate shithead punks like you. That old man comes from another country, but he's got just as much right as you do to live in this country."

"I never said he didn't."

"He's ten times the man you are. You're not even a man. You're a piece of shit. Just keep away from him. He can't hurt a fly. He don't even know his own name. You got a problem with your life? You bring it to the shrink. You got a problem with that old man? You bring it to me. You got that?"

Smith shut the door and fastened the locks. He was stunned at having been slandered and threatened. The brute's reliance on non sequitur had sucked all rationality out of the conversation. Why the hostility? Why the resentment? Did the boy's earliest memories include his being propped up on the windowsill overlooking the rose garden and taught to guard the street? Had he been told, Here is your future, here is who you are and all you will become? No wonder he scowled and glared and smoked cigarettes: In the window he had met his calling and his limit; his inheritance and sole privilege; the family heirloom, refined and transmitted from generation to generation; that which made him special and debased.

Smith worried about not being able to sleep because of the heat, because of the drilling next door, because of the upsetting conversations.

He walked into the kitchen and looked out the window. The night sky was cloudy. A blinking airplane descended toward a nearby airport. A car raced by in the street. In the window overlooking the garden, in the shifting light of the television hearth, piled on the ledge lay the forearms—not the mother's frozen set or the son's fleshy stubs but the primitive, trouble-making pair, one hairy limb of which stretched out to dislodge the invisible ash from the incandescent cigarette.

FOUR

"Things started out so smoothly," Smith lamented. "I moved in. I got settled."

"Trouble in paradise?" inquired Wendy, the waitress with the overbite.

"It feels more like hell, with this heat. Is every day as hot as this?"

"Usually it's hotter."

It was ten o'clock; with the breakfast rush over, he hoped Wendy would have time to chat.

"Neighbor problems," he explained. "Father and son. And wife. The son called me a liar."

"Well, are you?" She eyed him dubiously.

"No!" He was not amused. "This person accosted me last night."

"Really?" She shifted moods and looked concerned.

Smith glanced around nervously for eavesdroppers.

"He accused me of harassing his father, but actually it's the other way around: The father is harassing me. He looks like a caveman."

"With hairy arms, I suppose."

"Yes!"

"Like a spider."

"No, more like some kind of hybrid: half-man, half-ape. He was extremely impudent. He never saw me before and started talking to me and staring at me as if I were his long-lost son."

"So he's the father you never had," she quipped, teasing again. "Maybe number two son is jealous. What did daddy say?"

Smith shrugged. "I'm not exactly sure. Crazy things. I couldn't really understand him. He babbles. His English is awful. He's the janitor of the building where I'm staying. He mops the floors and takes out the trash, and the whole family sits in the window and watches the street."

"All at the same time?"

"No. They take turns. Not only that, but Saturday night the police came by and picked up the father for some reason."

"Maybe the floors were dirty."

He laughed at her irreverence, which made his story less pressing and helped him relax. She struck him as a tough and independent woman who did not get rattled easily, a rugged type; he imagined that for fun she rode motorcycles and parachuted out of airplanes.

"From what he tried to explain to me," Smith said, "I concluded that he might know something about a missing boy."

"I wouldn't lose any sleep over this," she advised. "Most people in this city are deeply disturbed. Don't let this guy bother you."

"I did see a poster with a picture of a missing child in the window of a bagel shop."

"That's just to attract attention and sell more bagels. What's this guy's sign?"

"His sign?"

"Yeah, his sign."

"His astrological sign? The father? I wouldn't know. I suspect he has no sign. He comes from a place where there are no signs."

She looked at him reproachfully but still in jest. "You shouldn't make fun of the heavens."

"Do they explain everything?"

"Enough to get me through the day." She tilted her head and looked at him anew.

His time had run out. "What'll it be?" She gripped her pencil and pad.

"A plain omelet and coffee."

Fresh customers had settled into booths. Wendy looked at the counter, where the cashier with the bushy mustache was eyeing her, as was the fat man with the mottled hands and watchdog face who occupied the same stool as the day before.

Wendy hurried to the cashier, and as the man whispered through his mustache, she nodded affirmatively.

From then on, she went full tilt, streaming in and out of the kitchen, racing behind the counter, zigzagging among the tables and booths. After a few minutes, she surged toward Smith with his dishes, clanged them down on the table and glanced at him to confirm that the food she brought was what he had ordered. Though the unexpected rush soon ended, she did not stop by his table again other than to drop off his bill as she hastened past, leaving it to the busboy to inquire whether he wanted more coffee. While recognizing the frenetic nature of her job, Smith blamed the cashier's whispered intervention for somehow having denied him Wendy's company. The fat man was again talking incessantly and now slipped from his stool and lumbered toward the bathroom in the back, granting a moment of calm to the cashier, who scanned the dining area. When his glance touched Smith's, when their eyes locked, the cashier averted his, pretending no contact had been made.

The day was hazy and muggy. Assuming he would accomplish little indoors, he left the restaurant and headed to Manhattan for sightseeing. That morning, he had thumbed through the tourist guide his sister had left for him and read a bit from the chapter covering the southern tip of Manhattan, an area the guide described as "the oldest section of the city," offering a park and "one of the finest panoramas of the harbor." From there he could walk to the World Trade Center, "the world's largest commercial complex, featuring New York's premier skyscrapers, twin 110-story towers rising skyward 1,350 feet, covering 16 acres." There were photographs of the Twin Towers, as well as of the Customs House, Wall Street, the Brooklyn Bridge. The book contained a map of the area with key attractions identified by numbers and black dotted lines plotting recommended walking tours. He then took out the subway map, which at first perplexed him, presenting a tangle of color-coded lines, numbers, letters; local stations, express stations, transfer points; countless opportunities for mistakes.

He stopped by the bagel shop, equipped with paper and pen, but the poster about the missing boy was gone, replaced by an announcement for a street festival. Smith wondered if that meant the poster child, whose name he had forgotten, had been recovered. And had he been found inside a box?

The subway ride began above ground, and at each station the car grew more crowded. Smith had taken a seat next to a man with heavy thighs who smelled like salami and was reading a newspaper. Teenage girls in short pants were standing in front of him, speaking Spanish, their legs almost brushing his knees. Between them he glimpsed an old, weary-eyed Chinese woman burdened by furrows in her forehead. Next to her sat a blond woman in sunglasses. Her shapely legs funneled to a pair of open-toed shoes with three-inch cork heels. On her bare knee was tattooed a drab purple butterfly.

The car filled up. Passengers squeezed together and maneuvered for space. A dark-skinned man in a baseball cap cursed under his breath while gripping for the handrail. "Excuse me!" "I'm sorry!" Heads shook impatiently. The air, which had been chillingly air-conditioned when Smith had first gotten on, now was warm and scented with bodies.

The train roared and rattled as it entered the tunnel. The wheels screeched against a bend in the tracks.

A peddler entered the car but could not wend his way through the crowd, so he gave his pitch by the door. He was selling sunglasses for one dollar a pair; an incredible price, he declared. No one acknowledged the solicitation.

"Excuse me. Is your name Michael?" asked the man who smelled like salami. He had rounded cheeks and a double chin.

"No," Smith replied. "It's not."

Without another word, the man returned to his news-paper and, at the next stop, got off without glancing back.

Smith transferred to a downtown express, rode eight more stops and detrained at Wall Street. He climbed a narrow staircase and emerged onto a street that roared with traffic and teemed with pedestrians. He walked down Broadway and viewed an old church and cemetery where were buried, according to his guidebook, "famous personages." What impressed him most, though, were the massive skyscrapers: glassy, blue-black giants reposed shoulder to shoulder high above the scurry of the over-shadowed streets. At one gilded entrance, workers churned through revolving doors, which never stopped turning.

It was lunchtime. The delis and sandwich shops were crowded. People walked in pairs or in clusters or rushed singly. Although many kept their eyes down, no two col-lided, and none looked lost or stumbled into a parking meter or a fire hydrant. Chips of conversation wafted past his ears: "What was she supposed to do?" "On the enamel. Do you believe that?" "Amplify, baby! Amplify!" For the most part, the voices were swamped by industrial noise: honking horns, shrieking brakes, police sirens, jackhammers, diesel engines. A city bus, like a flatulent geezer, sputtered to the curb and puffed gas in Smith's face. He alone was staggered by the assault; no one else gagged or covered his nose and mouth with a handkerchief. Standing against the stream was awkward, so he threaded a path along the curb, weaving around the meters and parking signs, straying too close to the traffic. Halted by a red light, he waited as the restlessness around him rose against the dam. Jaywalkers leaked into the street, challenging the traffic, darting through momentary breaks. One delivery man pushing a hand truck stepped off the curb without a pretense of caution while the cars and trucks dashed ahead, equally oblivious to the risks.

"Spare some change?" Next to him stood a panhandler who was wearing an overcoat despite the stifling heat. He presented Smith with a filthy, open hand. "Help me get something to eat." He wasn't wearing shoes; his feet were caked with black dirt. "A dollar?" he whimpered. He was trembling. "A dime? Anything you can spare?"

The traffic light changed; the onrushers flooded the crosswalk. Smith stayed where he was, pinned by the man's despairing eyes. He reached into his pocket, pulled out about seventy-five cents' worth of change and handed it over, freeing himself to scramble across the street. He looked back and saw the man thrusting his cupped hand at others who gave nothing and refused even to look. Here was an individual who had hit rock bottom, Smith observed. Had this wretched fellow once bustled with the crowd? Of what had he dreamed on his moving day?

Escaping the traffic and the steaming concrete, Smith entered Battery Park, with its lawns, London Plane trees and crowds of families and children, tour groups and loners. They carried cameras and backpacks; they besieged the hot dog stands and relaxed on the benches; they crossed the park in every direction; they wore T-shirts, baseball caps, cowboy hats, skullcaps; many had donned the green, foam-rubber crowns that were sold as souvenirs and mimicked the spiked headpiece of the Statue of Liberty. These toy crowns were especially popular among children, but adults laughed and joked with them, too.

While proceeding down a path between benches and cherry trees, Smith had the feeling of being followed but was unable to pick any particular face out of the proliferating crowd. Up ahead squatted Castle Clinton, a small, circular fort, described by his guide as "the sandstone centerpiece of the park"; at one time, cannons were positioned there and had guarded the harbor. Beyond it ran the promenade where vendors hawked drinks, food and souvenirs and where the harbor and the sky opened and expanded. Refreshing air blew off the choppy river, and just as he reached the railing the sun streaked through the haze and turned the water to a swift rolling shimmer of jewels dotted with motorboats and a long, slow barge. On the undulating surface diamonds of sun flickered like shards of broken glass. He leaned against the railing and looked out toward the famous statue. A ferry loaded with tourists had just pulled away from the dock.

To his right, in the water beyond the railing, on a stone platform secured by pilings, rose a memorial dedicated to the American merchant mariners. The sculpture depicted three men in the bow of a boat, which had tipped and was sinking. One of the mariners was kneeling, exhausted, his head sagging; a second was in a crouch, hands cupped to his mouth, calling for help or for responses from other survivors; a third lay across the gunwale, reaching down toward a fourth figure, who was overboard and reaching up out of the waves, calmly and rigidly, grasping vainly for the third man's proffered hand as the water lapped at his chest and throat. The guidebook gave no information about the memorial, but a plaque nearby dedicated the work to the "unrecognized thousands" of American merchant mariners who had "lost their lives at sea," sacrificing themselves "in pursuit of peaceful commerce." Sadly, the survivors sculpted there, in a scene inspired, the plaque explained, by an actual photograph taken during World War II, had perished in the catastrophe, "left to the perils of the sea," consigned to "the unmarked ocean depths" and realms other than their own.

He turned and watched the passersby, marveling at the abundant points of view that traversed the promenade in a single day, a single hour. The others, for the most part, failed to notice him though sometimes they looked his way, not at him directly but beyond him, over his shoulders, or at the ground around his feet. And yet he could not shake the feeling that at least one person's gaze was indeed trained on him.

A woman in a black dress and head scarf handed Smith a paper pamphlet, the cover of which showed a drawing of the Earth inside a black void. "Who created the world for you to live in?" the heading asked. "It was Jesus! For all things were created by him and for him." Inside pages had close-up drawings of angry mouths and frightened eyes and declared that Jesus knew how lonely and how scared every person was, that Jesus heard every word uttered, that Jesus understood every thought imagined, that all things and creatures and human beings stood revealed and naked before the eyes "of Him with whom we have to do."

Unconvinced, Smith dropped the pamphlet on the bench and left the park.

Following one of the maps in his book, he went up West Street, alongside a highway, in the direction of the World Trade Center. At Liberty Street, he crossed over and made his way into the crowds, past the vendors, and entered one of the Twin Towers through a revolving door.

Once inside, he gasped delightfully, succored by the air-conditioning, and gasped again as he turned full circle within the honeycombed shopping mall, admiring the expansiveness, the randomness, the relentless commerce. The shoppers and commuters darted so swiftly that Smith beheld just pieces: a jacket, a briefcase, a shopping bag, pale fingers lifting a cigarette, a child tossing trash in a can. Rarely did any two inadvertently touch.

An escalator carried him up to an outdoor plaza, back out into the sweltering heat, a discomfort he hardly noticed, for the twin colossal towers exploded into view, rocketing out of each other's shadow: flowing steel columns forking tridentally into tributaries that streamed farther up until they dazzled in the sun. While the impressive buildings on the narrower streets had drawn his attention but failed to rivet it, these towers mesmerized him. Later, he would learn from the guide how many square feet and how much plumbing each comprised, but for now he stared in awe of the monumental constructions, barely imagining beams sturdy enough to support such size yet unable to spot the tension, so fully was it hidden in the stillness and the form.

FIVE

By four that afternoon he was back in Queens at the coffee shop for an early dinner. He sat in a booth and let fatigue take hold of him momentarily. He closed his eyes, exhausted from the day's stimulation: the breezes of the harbor, the earthquakes of activity, the genius skyscrapers.

Wendy, apparently, was gone for the day, and Smith was left to the services of a sour-faced waitress with a smoker's gravelly voice. He asked for a recommendation. She shrugged—it was all the same to her—then blandly offered the pot roast. He chose the bluefish, which turned out dry and smelling like ammonia. He added salt but found nothing in the act—no genius there, just disappointed appetite.

From then on, he vowed, he would eat only eggs.

He entered his building from the south, at first keeping his head down in accord with policy, but again was unable to resist the urge to look up and see Dezmun in the window; in this case, it was the son, who was studying his fingernails and did not acknowledge Smith in any way. For the first time since moving day, Smith regretted living where he did. His sister was due back the first of September, and he was obligated to stay in the apartment until then, but he knew now that he needed to move, possibly across the river, preferably to a neighborhood with a park nearby; most importantly, to a building equipped with a doorman wearing a uniform, not a gargoyle wielding a mop.

He was dismayed as well by the quality and quantity of his interactions thus far with his neighbors. To his mild shock, he realized that the only persons with whom he had carried on sustained conversations were Kogat Dezmun and his ill-bred son. Surely there were others in that big building with whom he could make contact. Coming to mind was sweet-faced Carin, who had encouraged him to ask her for help. He decided to accept the offer, imagining her as a bored housewife who would look forward to his visit as a break from her tiresome routine. Exiting the elevator, he tiptoed down the hall, as though the visit were clandestine, and rang the doorbell to apartment 4F.

A woman's muffled voice responded through the door: "Who is it?"

"Your neighbor from 4B."

Locks were unbolted and the door opened a few inches, halted by a security chain. Through the gap, eye level with the taut chain, peered Carin's guarded face.

"I'm sorry to bother you," Smith said, "but I wondered if I could talk to you for a few moments."

She appeared not to recognize him.

"My name's Smith, from down the hall. We spoke briefly this past Saturday."

She clutched the chest of the terrycloth bathrobe she was wearing. "Is something wrong?" she asked.

"No, no. It's just that, besides you, I haven't really met anybody in the building, so, I was wondering, if you had a few moments, if we could talk a little bit, maybe I could ask you some questions about the neighborhood. Newcomer-type questions."

She considered his explanation. "Wait, please."

The door closed. Smith thought about leaving, assuming he had made a mistake by stopping by unexpectedly, but then the chain was unfastened, and the door opened all the way.

"Come in," Carin said, now dressed in slacks and a lime-green blouse.

Her apartment layout formed a reverse image of Smith's, with the kitchen immediately off the foyer but to the left instead of to the right, and the living room, bathroom and at least one bedroom in the back to the right.

He followed her into the kitchen. Potted plants covered the windowsill; teacups hung from hooks beneath the cabinet. On the tabletop, plastic placemats shaped a cartwheel with a bowl of oranges at the hub. By the time the two were seated and a kettle set on the stove, Carin had warmed up.

"I hope I'm not interfering with your dinner," Smith said.

"No, we are finished with dinner."

Smith glanced at the sink. There were no dirty pots or dishes, no food or indications of cooking. The table and placemats were perfectly clean.

"Are your children at home?"

"No, they are with their father. They will be here soon. Are you happy in your home now?" she asked, smiling and squinting cheerfully again.

"So far, so good."

She glanced at the kettle on the stove.

"Is this a bad time?" Smith asked.

"No, no. We can drink one cup of tea."

Though her English was fluent and correct, he detected an undefined accent: an overly chiseled articulation.

"It's a large building," he said. "Very impersonal. Hardly conducive to bringing people together, one on one, like this."

He noticed, when she smiled, a misaligned bottom tooth that, in his opinion, made her more attractive; by appearing less perfect she became for him more real.

The kettle whistled, and Carin poured two cups of cinnamon tea. She offered Smith half of a blueberry muffin, which he declined. As they sipped tea, and as Carin picked at the muffin, he told her about his arrangement with his sister regarding the apartment and his plans to

find his own place. Then they talked about the neighborhood: the available shopping, the transportation, the
relative security. As they talked, he heard the stiffness in
her pronunciation but hardly ever a grammatical or lex-
ical mistake. He then described his trip that day and how
impressed he had been.

"I saw thousands of people," he said. "At times I got
the feeling that each one believed he or she was the only
person that existed in the world."

They laughed.

Smith waited for Carin to speak, but she just set the
teacup down on the saucer. He used the pause to steer
the conversation back to the building and their neighbors. He told her about the old man who had turned his
back on him in the elevator.

"It is always good to say hello," she said firmly, then
spoke of a strong belief she had held since childhood; a
belief that all people, in their hearts, were basically
good.

"What about the janitor, Mr. Dezmun, the man who
mops the floors? What's his story?"

"What does this mean, 'his story'?" She sounded
concerned.

"Are you worried about living in the same building with
him?"

The question puzzled her. She put her hands in her
lap. "Mr. Dezmun is very friendly," she said.

"Yes, he's been very friendly to me, too," Smith confessed.
"But he's also given me some disturbing information."

"I tell my children, Mr. Dezmun says strange things, do not believe him sometimes." She started to smile, then a nervous look took hold of her eyes.

"I believe he's had trouble with the law," Smith said.

Again, she was concerned. "What does this mean 'with the law'?"

"With the police."

She answered sharply: "I think that was long ago."

"Not at all," Smith countered. "Last Saturday night. At about 11:45."

"I am sure it was nothing. Or something very small."

"By the way," he continued, "did you, by any chance, hear about a missing boy or read about a missing boy in the newspaper?"

Carin had lifted her cup and was about to sip, but now returned it untouched to the saucer.

"The boy was most likely kidnapped," Smith added.

"Oh my." She placed her hands in her lap.

"It happened recently," he said. "There was a report about it on the television news two nights ago, on Saturday. Did you see it?"

"Saturday we do not watch TV."

She turned the cup on the saucer so that the handle faced away from her. Then she turned it back.

"Well, have you heard anything at all about a missing child?" he asked.

"I don't remember. There are many stories like this on the television. I don't like to listen. It is very uncomfortable for me."

"So then you have seen stories like this. Do you re-member the names of any of the children?"

"No."

"Were they mostly boys or girls?"

"I don't remember."

"Do you remember what they looked like?"

"No."

She picked up her cup, touched the ceramic lip with her fingernail, put the cup back down, glanced at her wristwatch, then offered Smith a thin, nervous smile.

"You have two children?" he asked.

"Yes." She perked up. "My boy is six years, and my daughter is nine years. Do you have children?"

Smith laughed.

Carin seemed amused that her simple question had caught him off guard. "Do you want children?" she asked.

He thought a moment. "I'm not entirely sure."

"Children are wonderful," she beamed, adopting the role of the expert. "They bring joy, happiness, sunshine."

As she spoke, Smith admired her long white neck. At her temples, the blue veins, faintly visible, deepened her paleness.

"Yes, I suppose you're right," he conceded. "Children must be wonderful much of the time, but I can't help but shudder at the terrible anxiety you must suffer concern-ing their welfare."

"What does this mean, 'concerning their welfare'?"

"Don't you worry about your children's safety?"

She set the cup down with stark deliberateness. "Of course, I worry about my children's safety."

Smith had dug clumsily and offended her. He tried to explain: "I mean, with the numerous cases you've referred to."

"What does this mean, 'numerous cases'?"

"The missing children. Those stories you see on television."

"Mothers always worry about their children," she snapped.

"I assumed as much."

Disconcerted, she reached for the cup, then let it stand and placed her hands in her lap. "We cannot keep our children in a cage."

"Some people may be doing just that," Smith replied. "If not in a cage, then in a wooden box."

Her delicate features froze, enveloped by a stupefying silence.

He plunged ahead: "Has the janitor, Mr. Dezmun, ever talked to you about a boy in a box?"

A colder silence chilled an even more astonished face. She dropped her gaze, touched the cup, picked the cup up, put the cup down.

"You must not believe Mr. Dezmun very much," she said.

"He told me about a missing boy. Or at least a boy in danger. It's hard to know for sure. I can't understand what he's saying. His English is not very good. In fact, it's terrible. I'm certain, though, or almost certain that he said something about a little boy being kept in a wooden box."

"I do not understand anything like this." She spoke curtly, then sipped her tea, struggling to show composure.

"Why do Dezmun and his family sit in the window all the time and watch the street?" he asked.

"What is wrong with that?" She had turned sharply defensive, and Smith was stung by the shift in tone.

"Don't you find it disconcerting to be observed every time you come in or go out?" he asked.

"What does this mean, 'disconcerting'?"

"Confusing. Disturbing."

"They don't watch every time."

"Just about every time."

"It is what they do," she said, explaining nothing. "They are good neighbors."

"I might have agreed with you," he said, "were it not for this boy in the box."

Her hands trembled, and the cup and saucer rattled as she set them on the table. "If you know about this terrible thing, why don't you go to the police?"

"The police probably already know. As I said before, they took this man into custody."

"Then there is nothing more for you to say."

She seemed almost near tears.

"I'm sorry if you're upset," he said. "It's a gruesome story."

She stood up. "Excuse me. I must go." She removed the cups and saucers from the table and set them in the sink. "I must get ready," she explained. "Tomorrow I am going to a job interview."

"Is that a fact? What kind of a job?"

"Nothing special. An office job." She started out of the kitchen.

"Well, perhaps at some point in the near future we can exchange notes on job hunting," he suggested.

Carin agreed and led him into the foyer toward the door. As he left the apartment and the door slammed and locked behind him, Smith realized that her welcome had turned out to be less hospitable than her forthright invitation had promised.

SIX

That evening he sat watching television again in the prickly, draining heat. His stomach churned from the ammoniated bluefish, and gas bubbled up unpleasantly. After traversing the dial, he settled on a police drama. Two uniformed police officers were questioning a civilian who was nervous and defensive; the police remained calm and pretended to be the man's buddies. As the scene changed and the police entered a crowded bar to interview a younger man with tattooed arms, a soft rapping sounded from Smith's door. The janitor's son, he thought at first, but that dolt would have pounded. He turned off the television and slunk into the foyer but did not peek through the peephole, fearful of what he might find peering in.

He opened up. It was Kogat Dezmun: simian-gargoyle—black, mop-top hair; unblinking, overstimulated stare;

soda-bottle eyeglasses; a delighted, lascivious, presumptuous grin. He held his right arm behind his back.

"You see dem."

Smith noted the hand behind the back and suspected a weapon of some kind.

"You see dem," the janitor repeated.

"See whom?"

Dezmun uttered a word or phrase that Smith failed to understand. In a desperate search for vocabulary, the gargoyle backed up, still keeping his right hand behind him, pointed with his left hand at the radiator in the hall, then tapped the grill with a knuckle. "Idon."

"Iron?"

The janitor placed his free hand on his chest to indicate himself, then opened it to include Smith. "Men."

"Iron men?"

"Yes!"

"Look, Mr. Dezmun. Please believe me: I do not know what you are talking about." He spoke patiently and precisely but still watchful of the hidden hand. "I have not seen any iron men. I am certain of that."

"You see dem," Dezmun repeated, having grasped nothing, it seemed, of what Smith had explained. Then he said: "Boyd'bok."

Smith took a deep breath. "Mr. Dezmun, if you do know something about a boy in trouble, anything at all about a missing boy or a kidnapped boy, you must notify the authorities."

Dezmun did not understand.

"You must tell the police."

"No police!"

The prospect caused Dezmun anguish. He shook his head, waved his left hand; still, his right was concealed.

Smith had to be careful: What was this man holding?

"You see dem," Kogat repeated with conviction, returning to his iron men. "I see you."

Smith considered slamming the door in the man's face. "Where do these iron men live?" he asked instead.

Kogat Dezmun curled his left palm as if holding an imaginary sphere. "Inside."

"Inside what?" Smith was aware that Dezmun might have misused the preposition, might have intended the notion of "on" or "over" or "around" or any number of relational concepts. "Inside a ball? Inside a house? Inside a grocery store?"

"No, no." The janitor screwed his face as if tasting something sour.

"Where then? In the ocean?"

"Yes!" Kogat glowed.

Smith pictured submarines or sunken cauldrons or discarded beer cans though these were made of aluminum. "Look, it's late. I have to get ready for bed. I expect to be extremely busy the next few days. I haven't slept all that well the past couple of nights, partly, I must say, because of you. Maybe you can talk to somebody who can understand you better because I can't. Now, I'm sorry, but I must say good night."

Dezmun followed Smith's moving lips with fascination, apparently paying little heed to the content of his words, all the while maintaining his hand behind his back, until now, when, without warning, like a suitor's outstretched arm delivering a bouquet, his right hand swung out from behind him and bestowed on Smith a green, foam-rubber Statue of Liberty crown.

Smith accepted the offering, but he could not speak; he was helplessly mute. His eyes pleaded with the gargoyle.

Dezmun placed one hand gently over the other, pressed both firmly to his breast, covering his heart, closed his eyes, sighing and smiling tranquilly, signifying love: He had done it for love, he announced in mime. All he did he did for love. Next, he went into a crouch, slightly bending his knees, and put his cupped hands to his mouth, shouting without making a sound.

Smith slammed the door, which echoed through the hall, echoed more thunderously than any slammed door he had heard before. He stood rooted to the spot, his stomach rigid like a rock, shuddering at the horror. For all he knew, Kogat Dezmun was still on the other side of the door, frozen in that sailor's pose, just like the statue in Battery Park. With his hands Smith kneaded the souvenir headpiece. The gargoyle had followed him to the park. The scene as he recalled it had been transformed. From the canvas of points and facets, from among the ferries and the trees, the vendors and the tourists, from the wild stew of moments and particulars, there now lunged forward, as if all else had been washed away, a single detail: the memorial to the American merchant mariners. Stricken sailors in the tipped bow of a sinking boat. *Iron men.* One on his knees; one reaching over the gunwale toward another drowning in the waves, their fingers almost touching; and one, with knees bent, hands cupped to his mouth, shouting without making a sound, calling for help or for the whereabouts of other stranded souls, knowing that his cries, if ever rendered audible, would be blown back into his face or pulled beneath the water to the unmarked ocean depths.

SEVEN

"I need advice," Smith pleaded.

"Concerning breakfast, I hope."

Wendy stood poised with pencil and pad.

"It's deeper than that."

"Then you'll have to wait."

She took his order and went to the kitchen. Smith had settled into the second booth, his regular spot. In other booths a couple hunched over coffee and a businessman sopped eggs with bread. At the counter, the fat man was absent, and on his stool a little girl whirled while her mother placed an order to go. The cashier was gazing from his post at the register, and Smith imagined playfully that the mustache was a fake, a prop for the atmosphere.

He lingered with his coffee, thumbing through the newspaper. Headlines announced a quintuplet birth, a small plane collision, a hotel fire, a $65 million lottery prize. But while offering a two-page spread on the five newborn babies, it said nothing about the Sanderson boy or any other missing child.

He paid his bill, left the restaurant and walked once around the block. When he returned, he found Wendy outside on her cigarette break.

"Busy morning," he remarked.

Wendy agreed. Her mood was muted, subdued, drained of adrenaline.

"Awfully hot," he said.

She exhaled smoke.

"When you're working," he commented, "you look like a matador."

Wendy chuckled. "Sometimes I feel like I'm facing wild bulls. What do you do?"

"I'm an industrial designer."

"Oh, really!"

"I design consumer products."

"You mean," she hesitated, "you take something that works and make it more complicated."

"On the contrary: I make it better by modifying it, preferably by simplifying it."

"You reinvent the wheel."

Smith laughed. "Thanks for the idea. Actually I work with details, the tiny things that we tend to overlook but that make life easier."

"I like those tiny things." She took a drag on her cigarette and watched the traffic.

"I work on everyday utility items."

"Really? Like household appliances?"

"Yes, for example."

"You aspire to build a better toaster?" Her voice trailed up incredulously.

He laughed. "I've never considered a toaster, but thanks for another idea. No, actually, I've done some work on a garbage can lid and a dustpan, among others."

Wendy eyed him uncertainly. With her lips closed, she ran her tongue along her overbite.

"Dustpan and garbage can?" she asked.

"Garbage can lid."

"Of course. The lid. Among others."

"For instance, I'm excited about an idea I had yesterday afternoon. For a new eyeglass case."

"Not the glasses, just the case."

"First I focus on the case." He laughed at his unintended pun.

"And you like this work?" she asked, her voice rising doubtfully, as if hoping Smith were making a joke.

"I love it." He looked directly at her to show he was in earnest. She glanced away to drag on the cigarette. He described his previous day's visit to Manhattan, how he had been struck by the skyscrapers and all the activity, how he had wondered whether every detail, including the smallest of gestures or of objects, was in fact indispensable to the whole. What if, he asked, at an earlier time, a waitress in a coffee shop had flicked a cigarette with her left hand instead of with her right? Would the ensuing profusion of altered details have modified all that followed? Would those gigantic skyscrapers be standing exactly where they were? Would they be standing at all? Might he and Wendy not have wound up standing where they were, at that moment, talking to each other?

"You know what?" Wendy asked, exhaling smoke. "You think too much."

"Is it possible to think too much?"

"Oh, it's possible."

At his probing, she talked about herself. She lived around the corner, was originally from Maryland, where it was even hotter than in New York. She wanted to be an actress and was taking classes.

She looked at her watch. "I have to go back soon."

"Remember that man I told you about yesterday morning?"

"You mean your adopted father?"

"He's creepy. The whole family is creepy. These aren't sympathetic people."

Wendy took a final drag on her cigarette, then dropped it and crushed it with the toe of her sneaker.

"Yesterday, without my knowledge, the old man followed me to Battery Park and, to prove that he had been there and had seen me, brought me back a souvenir. One of those foam-rubber Statue of Liberty crowns."

"Oh, yeah! I like those crowns."

"Well anyway, I think he told me that he loved me."

"Oh, really! Did he get down on one knee?"

Smith cringed remembering the ghastly scene. "No, he didn't kneel, but he did use gestures, crossing his hands on his heart and sighing." Smith demonstrated. "Like that."

"Don't trust gestures," she warned.

"What do you think about dreams?" he asked.

She seemed surprised by the change of theme. "What do I think about dreams? Everything! I dream for dreams." She glanced at her watch.

"Do they mean anything?"

"Everything means something."

"Then listen to this dream. I was on a sunny street in Chinatown. A run-down area. I know it was Chinatown though I didn't see any Chinese people. There was broken glass everywhere. I came to an alleyway, and standing there, looking out at me, was a peddler offering to sell me a wooden box. The kind they pack oranges in."

"Don't they use cardboard to pack oranges?"

"Maybe. Anyway, this was a wooden crate. About three feet high and two feet wide. He wanted to sell it to me. He didn't say anything, but he opened the side of the box—it had a little door with a handle—and inside was a small boy, maybe three or four years old, completely boxed in. His little arms and little legs were doubled up, and his neck and head were crammed in a corner. There was blood on his face, and his eyes were black and blue and almost shut. I realized with a shock that the boy was still alive. Anyway, that's when I woke up, and, as you might imagine, I couldn't go back to sleep."

As she listened, Wendy stiffened. "I have to go," she said.

"The janitor planted that dream in my head," Smith complained. "That was the missing boy he had tried to tell me about. I mentioned that to you yesterday. Remember?"

"This janitor sounds too strange," she replied, again glancing at her watch.

"You may be right. Still, I can't be certain that what he's saying is completely untrue. Maybe this boy he talks about is the same boy that was reported missing on the news a few nights ago, the Sanderson boy."

"That's unlikely."

"But it's possible. The story was broadcast last Saturday night."

"Those cases are rarely what they appear to be at first. The parents are splitting and one of them grabs the kid, or the kid just gets so fed up by all the crap at home, he runs off for a couple of days."

"This boy was only four years old. He wouldn't have run away. And on television I saw both parents together."

"Everything on television is distorted."

He persisted: "Even if this boy in the box is not the Sanderson boy, he could be another missing boy."

"He's a boy that you dreamed up."

"What about the janitor's story?"

She shook her head. "Trust me. In the end, the child always turns up."

"Always?"

She shrugged. "Most of the time."

Smith was surprised by her lack of curiosity. "Even if, in the end, most missing children reappear, 'most children' means at least one child still missing, in the end, as it were, in which case we have a responsibility to do something."

"Why are you telling me about this?" she snapped, suddenly cross. "If you're so concerned about this dream you had . . ."

"It's not just the dream."

"It doesn't matter. The question is: Why are you telling me about it? Tell the police. Don't expect me to play detective."

There was a knock from inside on the coffee shop window: The busboy was indicating to Wendy that her break had lasted too long.

"I have to go."

She started inside.

"Can we talk some more later?"

"I don't think so." She glanced at him apologetically, her hands on her hips. "We really don't have all that much in common."

EIGHT

This time Smith stuck with policy and did not look at the janitor's window though he felt himself watched as he entered the vestibule of his building. Inside, the welcome mat had been stood up against the door, and the floor in the lobby was drying; the wetness of the mop left a trail on the tiles like the swipe of a lizard's tail.

The gargoyle was at large.

Smith made a decision: His hide-and-seek policy was silly; he would no longer hurry up the stairs or slink into the elevator to avoid unpleasant neighbors. Every time he came or went, regardless of the direction, he would look squarely at whichever gargoyle was looking at him. Determinedly, he marched to apartment 1G. The buzzer was not functioning, so he knocked heavily, listened a moment, knocked again less loudly; then came the unlockings, and the cavern opened up.

Mrs. Dezmun stood in front of him in her shabby black dress, with her frog eyes showing nothing: no surprise, no discomfort, no emotion of any kind. Her skin was flaky and, in spots on the cheeks, close to purple. He noted the mole and the gray hair and the mustache. He introduced himself as the subtenant in 4B and asked if Mr. Kogat Dezmun was available to speak with him. She replied, "No." He asked if she knew when Mr. Dezmun might return. She answered, "No." He asked if she knew where he might be, and again she told him, "No." Finally he instructed her, politely and with a smile, to inform Mr. Dezmun that he, Smith, the subtenant in apartment 4B, had stopped by and wished to talk to him. For a final time, to his surprise, without the rudeness that the rejoinder should have conveyed, she presented him a simple "No."

Vexed and frustrated, he walked up the stairs. On the fourth floor, as he proceeded down the corridor, keys in hand, he encountered another gargoyle but not the one he had asked for. The teenage Dezmun, in denim overalls and carrying an electric hand drill, had stepped out of apartment 4C and was locking the door.

"Excuse me," Smith said, noticing the drill. "Has there been drilling going on in that apartment during the night?"

"You got a problem with that?"

"Yes, I do, as a matter of fact." Smith tried not to sound confrontational. "You see, while you're drilling, I'm next door trying to sleep. The drilling keeps waking me up."

"Yeah, well, I'm all finished." He pressed for the elevator and stood there winding the cable around the handle of the drill.

With keys poised, Smith paused in front of his door; he hesitated, tempted to speak. "There's something else I'd like to talk to you about," he said.

The young man glared.

"About your father."

"We had an agreement."

"You said if I had a problem with your father, I should take it to you."

"Yeah, well, I changed my mind. Now I'm telling you to stay away from me."

He let the cable, which he had completed winding around the drill handle, drop loose, then started winding it again. On his left wrist he wore a silver watch with a leather band.

"Look. I just want to talk," Smith explained.

"Why should I talk to you?" The boy sneered. He kept his eyes on the winding cable. "What do you think? I got nothing better to do than talk to you? You want to talk to me?" He looked up, challenging Smith with his jaw. "You make it worth my while."

Smith understood. "I'll give you ten bucks," he offered.

The cable dropped; the boy's scowl collapsed, and for an instant he became a child awed by an adult's audacity. "You want to give me ten bucks?"

"In exchange for the opportunity to ask you questions about what your father said to me."

He eyed Smith askance. "Let me get this straight: You're going to give me ten bucks to ask me questions?"

"About what your father said to me."

"About what my father said to you?"

"That's right. Of course, I'll expect you to answer them."

"Answer what?"

"The questions I ask you."

"About what my father said to you."

Smith said nothing, realizing he was being mocked.

The elevator had come and gone, so young Dezmun pressed for it to return, then resumed rewinding the cable around the drill handle. His head was tilted back tauntingly. "What if I don't want to answer your questions?"

"You'll be obligated to."

The boy laughed. "Who's going to make me?"

Smith took a breath, hoping to avoid confrontation.

"Listen," the boy started. "If you want to ask me questions about what my father said to you, you got to put up more than ten bucks." He glared triumphantly, turning the cable.

Smith responded: "Ten dollars, that's all."

"I want fifty."

"Fifteen."

"For fifteen minutes."

At the end of the hall, a woman in a bathrobe shuffled out and dropped trash down the disposal chute before waddling back to her apartment.

"In here." The son unlocked apartment 4C and ushered Smith inside. The floor plan was the same as Carin's, mirroring Smith's apartment. The rooms were empty and the walls freshly painted. With the window closed, there was no ventilation, and the air was stuffy and smelled of paint. Both the boy and Smith were sweating.

"Someone moving in?" Smith asked.

Dezmun faced Smith in the foyer. "Fifteen bucks," he demanded, then glanced at his watch.

"I'll give you five dollars now, the other ten when we're done."

"Cut the crap. I get fifteen bucks right now, or the deal's off."

"Just a moment ago you suggested that you might be unwilling to answer my questions. I'll let you have the full fifteen when we're finished."

The youth glared, gripping the drill like a handgun, but he did not refuse the five dollars that Smith handed over. He stuffed the money into a front pocket of his overalls. "Now let's have the other ten."

"First we talk."

"No way!" He was sharp and firm. "Ten dollars right now, or we're done!"

"If you leave," Smith insisted, "you have to give me back that five-dollar bill."

"No way!" Young Dezmun laughed and looked at his watch. "You already wasted one minute."

"We haven't started yet!" Smith protested.

"Sure we have." The boy looked at his watch. "One minute, eight seconds. Now if you don't want to waste that five spot, hand over the other ten right now and start asking me your moron questions."

_s_ , cornered. The porky Dezmun smirked,
 cable, nonchalant, with all the time in the

us wallet, Smith withdrew and surrendered a
ar bill.

/ we go inside?" he gestured toward the kitchen,
/ offered space and light and some air if the window
opened. "It's probably cooler in there."

ezmun ignored the request, preferring the dim foyer
ere they stood crammed face-to-face. He looked at his
atch. "Thirteen minutes to go," he announced.

"What's your name?" Smith asked.

"Lupo."

"Lupo? Where are you from?"

"Downstairs."

Smith frowned. "That's not what I meant. I'm not paying for sarcasm."

"Yeah, I know. You're paying to ask questions about
what my father said to you." He glanced at his watch.

"Well, then: your father. Where is he from?"

"He's dead."

"Excuse me?"

"You heard me."

"Your father's dead?"

"You got a problem with that?"

"Your father's not dead."

The boy stiffened and reared. "Who the fuck are you to
tell me my father's not dead?"

"The janitor, Kogat Dezmun, is not dead."

"He's not my father. He's my uncle."

Smith was confused. "You said he was your father."

"I never said he was my father. *You* said he was my father."

"No." Smith shook his head. "Two nights ago you said he was your father."

"Are you calling me a liar?"

"I'm simply saying that two nights ago you said he was your father."

"Never mind two nights ago. He's my uncle, and that's the end of that." Lupo glanced at his watch. "Now what other moron questions you got?"

Smith assessed his interlocutor: a perspiring hog conniving in a shadowy, cramped, stiflingly hot, newly painted sty. "You know," Smith said, "this damages your credibility."

Lupo sneered and let the cable unwind.

"Let me remind you," Smith said. "I've paid you for information. That counts for something here."

"That don't count for crap. That just means you're a moron."

Smith was sweating. "Can't we go inside and open the windows?"

Lupo said nothing, winding the cable more carefully so that the rings were even and did not overlap.

"Look," Smith said. "I was told a very disturbing story, and I'm just trying to find out what it's all about so I can do what's right."

"Giving some guy you don't know fifteen bucks to ask him questions about his dead father? You call that doing what's right? I call that being a punk and a pervert." He looked at his watch. "And a moron. Ten minutes to go."

Smith took a deep breath, drawing on his patience. He wiped the perspiration from his neck and his forehead. "Let's, for the sake of this discussion, assume that Kogat Dezmun's your uncle. The man appears to be a conscientious worker, always mopping the halls or carrying out the trash, but in the time I've been living here, which amounts to about three full days, that man has also been harassing me, or, if harassing is too strong a word, he's been bothering me, or, if that's too strong, let's just say he's been behaving toward me in an unexplained and peculiar manner. For instance, yesterday, he followed me to a park in Manhattan. Now why did he do that?"

"How should I know." Lupo replied, winding the cable. Then he shrugged. "What else do you want to know?"

"Why does he presume to know me?"

"Maybe he knows you."

"He doesn't know me."

"Maybe he does. Maybe you met him once, a long time ago, and you just don't remember."

"That's not possible."

"What more do you want me to say?" Lupo hitched his shoulders and looked at his watch. "Eight and a half minutes."

"I think he called me alabaster boy. What does that mean?"

Again Lupo merely shrugged.

"I saw the police pick him up the other night," Smith said. "What did he do?"

"That's none of your business."

"Then why have I paid you fifteen dollars?"

"Beats the piss out of me. Why?"

"To answer my questions!"

"Oh yeah, about what my father said to you. But I told you, he's not my father. He's my uncle."

Continuing seemed pointless, but Smith refused to throw away the time he had purchased. "Who are the iron men?" he asked.

Lupo looked puzzled.

"Kogat Dezmun talked to me about iron men. What did he mean?"

"How should I know?"

"I suspect that by iron men Mr. Dezmun was referring to a certain monument at Battery Park, a memorial to merchant mariners who were lost at sea."

"If you say so," Lupo replied incongruously, placidly winding the cable.

"Does Kogat Dezmun talk to statues?"

"I'll tell you this: Him talking to statues makes a lot more sense than me talking to you."

Smith sensed that he was talking to himself. "You haven't answered my question."

"Why should I? You already know the answer. You know all the answers." Lupo looked at his watch. "Seven minutes."

A protest would only waste time. "Is there somebody called the one true beggar?"

"There's a one true pervert. I know that."

"What about the boy in the box?"

Lupo lowered his arms and let the cable dangle onto the floor. "What are you talking about?"

"Your father said . . ."

"Hey!" Suddenly fierce, he pointed the drill at Smith's face, closing one eye as if taking aim. "For the last time, I'm telling you, the man is not my father!"

Smith stepped back and glimpsed, in the kitchen, a square of light that had fallen from the window and was brightening the wooden floor. They should have been talking in the kitchen, but Lupo would not budge.

"Okay," Smith conceded. "Kogat Dezmun—your father or your uncle, you decide—told me something about a boy in a box. I don't know what he meant. I don't know whether he was referring to an actual boy in an actual box or not. So tell me, Lupo, what did he mean?"

Lupo lowered the drill and grasped the cable. "The old man says a lot of crazy things." He had softened his voice and became a boy again in the gloomy foyer. "But you paid to ask me questions about my father, not about my uncle."

"You're not getting any more money," Smith said, suspecting a ploy.

"Well, I ought to."

Smith persisted: "Is there an actual boy in an actual box?"

"What do you think?" Lupo scrutinized Smith through narrowed eyes. He held the cable by the three-prong plug as if gripping the head of a snake.

Smith said nothing.

Lupo looked at his watch. "You got six minutes."

"Is that what the police questioned Kogat Dezmun about?" Smith asked.

"About what?"

"The boy in the box! Did the police the other night question Kogat Dezmun, the janitor, your uncle, about the boy in the box?"

"How should I know? Why don't you go down to the police station and ask them yourself?"

"Maybe I should."

"Maybe you should. They're your friends."

Smith pressed the point: "Look. A life might be at stake."

"Not your life. Why should you give a shit?"

Smith stared, dumbstruck by the boy's callousness. He stammered: "There may be a missing boy out there!"

"Out where?"

"Out there, in the world!"

"There ain't no missing boy out there," Lupo declared, then looked at his watch. "Five minutes."

"I know you're playing a game," Smith said. "And I know I can't win. Let me just state this for the record, as it were: There was a news report on television three nights ago about a boy who had disappeared from in front of his home. Your uncle, on three separate occasions, attempted to describe to me the figure of a naked boy in a wooden box. What exactly that means, whether there is a connection between this figure described by your uncle and that missing child reported on TV or some other child, I do not know."

Lupo's right hand held the cable, his left hand clutched the drill; both were motionless. His mocking glance had hardened into wariness. "You are one sick punk perverted piece of shit," he pronounced.

Smith fumed. "Why are you being so closed-minded? Why in the world would I go to all this trouble if I did not sincerely believe a serious matter were at hand?"

"Because you're a piece of shit. Because you're a punk. Because you think you're so much smarter than everybody else. Because you'll do whatever it takes to make somebody else feel stupid."

"That's not true."

"I know your type," Lupo went on. "You think nobody else understands what you're talking about. You think you're the only one who's smart enough to understand and everybody else is too stupid. But you're the real moron, hung up on what some crazy old man whispers into your ass, and you don't even know what he's saying."

Smith's shoulders sagged. "I'm just trying to do the right thing," he muttered.

"That's it." Lupo became animated, wound the cable around the handle of the drill with abrupt deliberateness, then tucked the plug under the coil to keep it in place. "This shit we got going on is over." He moved to the door and opened it. "Get out!"

Smith protested. "I've got time left."

"You got crap! You broke the rules. Now get your sick ass out of this apartment!"

"I demand a refund."

"Get out!"

Smith refused to finish the fight. He stepped out into the hall, and behind him the door to apartment 4C slammed shut.

He had wasted his money. For fifteen dollars he had bought hostility, chicanery, mendaciousness. On the other hand, he had learned that the boy was not the tough he pretended to be; he only mimicked a gangster, with bluff and cigarettes. He was rude, sneaky and thievish but no brute. And now Smith knew his name; the pudgy gargoyle was called Lupo, and by learning the name and by pronouncing it, Smith had softened him. He judged the boy as both smarter and more asinine than he had imagined him to be, but made of flesh, not cut from stone.

As to other issues, matters of substance and science—as to the boy in the box—Smith had learned nothing at all. On most points, Lupo lacked believability. Surely, two nights ago, he had called Kogat Dezmun his father, and, unless gargoyles were inbred, which, to Smith, was not inconceivable; unless at some point between Sunday night and Tuesday afternoon Lupo's father had married Lupo's aunt, to assert that in fact the man was his uncle, provoked in Smith the deepest doubt. And even if Smith had falsely remembered the earlier conversation and indeed Lupo had never stated that Kogat was his father but had simply not denied the relationship, still the younger Dezmun had certainly lied when denying the most salient and obvious of truths: that at least one child, somewhere in the world, at any particular moment, accidentally or otherwise, had separated from his mother and his father, from his babysitter or from his kindergarten teacher, and had disappeared, had been declared missing, was undeniably, perhaps irretrievably, lost. A mere minute inside the raucous city would convince the most blithely optimistic observer that similar displacements, mislocations, vanishings or thefts were inevitable. And if Lupo had lied about what was so apparent, had he lied as well when dismissing his father-uncle as a crazy old man whose pronouncements would best be ignored?

That night was the most humid of the four nights thus far, and Smith had no desire for television. Instead, to prepare for his interview, he sat at his desk, despite the heat, and commenced a series of visualization exercises. On the yellow pad, he sketched what he predicted he would see upon entering the office in which the interview would take place. He drew a rectangle for a desk, two triangles for chairs, a smaller rectangle for a window, a pair of stick figures. He then closed his eyes and pictured the room. But when he tried, in his mind, to embody the stick figure he placed behind the desk, the shape remained two-dimensional and unimagined, neither man nor woman, a shape with just a name—Dr. Weber—and a purpose.

His concentration flagged. The heat made him dizzy. He got up, went into the kitchen, looked out the window. The sky was overcast. Beneath the clouds, an airplane coasted down. In the street, a car sped by, headlights beaming. The gargoyles were home, of course: There were elbows on the sill, bathed in the television glow, but the torso was recessed, and Smith could not determine which cretin was on duty.

He returned to the desk and the yellow pad but could escape neither the phrase nor the image: *the boy in the box*. He could not dismiss what he had heard: that a boy was imprisoned in a box. He could not evade the child's pain, the child's anguish, his shocking aloneness, his wretched compression, all of which Smith found past enduring. Nor could he substantiate the information, assess its value, declare the figure a fantasy or a fact. Both Wendy and Carin had suggested that he go to the police. Even Lupo had challenged him to inform the authorities. All three had exhibited impatience, even annoyance, with Smith's curiosity, as if his concern had, to borrow Lupo's expression, broken the rules.

He had to do his duty as a citizen and as a human being. The next day he would visit the police and tell them what he knew. If his information were of no use to their investigation, they would dispose of it properly. Why should he lug it around on his conscience?

He had hoped to construct an uncomplicated life, just to get himself going. He had purposely selected unobstructed lines, the easiest of angles, avoided ravels and arabesques. He had planned on displaying responsibility, obeying the law, fitting in, doing right by others and, in return, receiving respect and a place to be. He recognized that living in a big city would force him to share space with odd and deviant personalities, but the insolent, crazy-eyed, incoherent janitor had gone too far, had barged in on his space, had raised confusion, had mucked things up, and Smith, his stomach tensing, fury tightening in his chest, resented the intrusion.

He took a shower, but his skin was soon sticky and tingly again and remained so through the entire uncomfortable night. Once in bed, his mind drifted sleepily, pulling him down—a damp, deranged and troubled descent—dropping him onto a carousel of painted gargoyles, wooden elephants and horses with hideous grins. The platform rotated, the gears and shafts creaked and churned, but the scenery stayed the same, turning and returning, until a hammering from the apartment next door yanked him back to wakefulness and staring into the dark.

NINE

Just two stories high, made of beige brick and gray cement, the precinct station was a citadel with gates on the windows and a palisade of cruisers parked diagonally out front. In the air-conditioned vestibule were cinder block walls painted two shades of blue, plastic chairs, a public telephone, a bulletin board posting announcements. Two closed doors had signs on the lintels: the Community Room and the Complaint Room.

At the front desk a policewoman in uniform had just hung up the phone. Behind her a man in street clothes was leafing through a file.

"I'd like to speak with someone concerning a possible missing child."

The man in street clothes looked up from the file.

The policewoman's hair was pulled back in a tight knot, and she looked at Smith inquiringly. "You want to report a missing person?"

Smith was unsure how to reply. "Well, more specifically, a missing child, a missing boy, actually. Most specifically, I wish to relay a report I received about a missing boy."

"What's the boy's name?"

"I don't know. I was given some information regarding him, but my source may not be reliable."

The officer frowned. Her task involved assessing the credibility of witnesses walking in off the street, and to that end she studied Smith skeptically.

"What's this other person's name?" she asked.

"You mean the unreliable source? Kogat Dezmun. He's the janitor in my building."

"Write it down."

She handed him a memo pad and a pencil. He leaned the pad against the wall and wrote.

"I'm not sure I spelled the first name correctly. The last name I saw on the intercom directory."

She took the pad and read aloud—"Ko-Gat Dez-Mun"— then tore the sheet off.

"Take a seat in there." She gestured toward the Complaint Room.

"I don't have a complaint," he said.

She eyed him with restraint. "It's just a place to wait."

The Complaint Room was dusty and cluttered with metal shelves burdened by papers and folders, telephone books, clipboards and boxes of ballpoint pens. There were filing cabinets, a discarded computer, a foot ladder, even a mop and a broom. A small, barred window high on the wall allowed in a lattice of light.

Smith, the only complainant present, sat down on a plastic bucket-seat chair.

On the wall hung a bulletin board covered by announcements, memos and newspaper clippings, the most recent notices obscuring the earlier ones. From his vantage point sitting down, the only message he could read was pinned to the middle of the board; a black and white sign in block letters spelling a single word: "THINK."

Soon the man in street clothes appeared holding the sheet of paper, on which Smith had written Kogat Dezmun's name. He introduced himself as Detective Poland.

Smith stood, and they shook hands. Detective Poland had a long face, lingering strands of disappearing hair, an arched nose turned down like the beak of a bird. The beak was stuffed, apparently, for the man breathed noisily through his gaping mouth. He was wearing a white shirt and a striped navy tie loosened at the collar and did not appear to be carrying a gun.

"Kogat Dezmun," the detective read from the paper he was holding. "I know the name well. What's the problem?"

"He's the janitor of my building, and he told me something that I thought might be useful to one or more of your investigations."

Poland stopped him from saying another word by holding up his palm. "My advice to you is to forget about this Kogat Dezmun. He's a nut-job. He's not dangerous, though. Don't let him get to you."

"I assumed he was unstable," Smith concurred. "At the same time, though, I have to admit the possibility that what he said to me might provide an important fact or perspective that could contribute to the closing of a case."

"Leave the case closings to us," Poland urged abruptly. He was Smith's height and looked him squarely in the eyes. "Everything's being handled properly." He flashed a packaged smile, tight with nervous energy. "This individual's not connected to any case whatsoever. As a matter of fact, we had him in here a few nights ago."

"Yes, I know. I saw him being put into a police car. I wondered whether it had something to do with the Sanderson boy, the missing boy I saw reported about on the news."

"Never mind the news. You won't learn anything from the news. As I said, every case is being handled properly." Poland flattened the loose hair across his scalp. "It's highly improbable that Kogat Dezmun told you something that he didn't tell us."

"'Highly improbable' implies 'slightly probable'. If it's slightly probable, it might be worth investigating."

Poland tilted his head forward and peered, fatigued, over the beaked nose. His voice became edgier. "I told you already: The guy doesn't know anything. He did something years ago, so we keep an eye on him. That's all. Now go home and forget about him." He tried lightening the mood. "Are you married?" he asked.

"No!" Smith laughed.

"Then go find a nice young lady, have a little fun." He took Smith by the shoulders and steered him toward the door.

Smith resisted. "You know, detective, with all due respect, I'm puzzled by your reluctance even to hear what I have to say. I believe it's possible, highly unlikely perhaps but nevertheless possible, that this man told me something that you don't know about. He described a graphic and disturbing picture."

"Is it just a picture?"

"I don't know the answer to that."

Poland compressed his lips, puffed up his wide cheeks, then let the air stream out. With his jaw hanging open, his face looked stretched, his forehead pulled forward. "Wait here," he said and left the room.

Smith remained standing and examined up close the newspaper clipping on the bulletin board. "Cops on Wheels" read the headline, and a picture showed two policemen patrolling the neighborhood on bicycles. The first paragraph quoted the glowing opinions held of the police officers by a group of senior citizens.

"Let's go in here."

Detective Poland had returned and was unlocking the Community Room.

As in the rest of the precinct, the cinder block walls of the Community Room were two-toned blue: dark cobalt from the waist down, cerulean up to the ceiling where tubular fluorescent bulbs cast a harsh, vibrating light. The room was as cool as a basement, with the air-conditioning set too high. An unused desk was pushed against the wall; otherwise, there were no folders or coffee cups strewn about, no shelves, no bulletin board; just the desk and a stack of metal folding chairs, three of which Detective Poland arranged triangularly in the middle of the room.

A third man came in and closed the door. He was Detective Brinkman, a corpulent black man with a light, freckled complexion, a toothbrush mustache, and short, curly hair flecked with gray. His hazel eyes were friendly and intelligent. He had no jacket on and was wearing a beige short-sleeve shirt that hugged his rotundity too tightly, making a bulge of his stomach and smaller ones of each breast. A cellular telephone was clipped to his belt, sheathed like a pistol.

Smith and Brinkman each took a chair while Poland remained standing, arms akimbo. Brinkman laid his left leg over his right knee, then clasped his left knee with his joined hands. "We have assembled!" he announced histrionically.

Poland shrugged as if asking why.

"It's cold in here," Smith said.

"And hot out there," Brinkman replied. "It's like a furnace out there."

"It's hell out there," Poland added.

"Can you turn down the air-conditioning?" Smith asked.

"It's central air," Poland submitted. "Nothing we can do."

Smith took a breath and launched his narration, mostly addressing Brinkman but glancing now and then at Poland, who appeared relieved to have ceded the primary role. Smith explained that he had arrived four days earlier from the West Coast and was subletting his sister's apartment, that he had come to this city to find a job in industrial design and, in fact, had an interview scheduled for the following day, that almost immediately upon arriving in his sister's building, he had been approached by the janitor.

Poland handed Brinkman the paper with Dezmun's name on it.

"He accosted me in the hallway, acted as if he knew me, called me 'alabaster boy', whatever that means, followed me to Battery Park. He even suggested, quite disturbingly from my point of view, through miming and gestures, that he loved me in some way."

"Ko-Gat Dez-mun," Brinkman read. "He's some foreign guy down on 37th Street, right?"

"36th Street," Smith corrected.

"Thick glasses? Head full of hair?"

"That's him!" Smith felt reassured. "He may know something about a missing child. I saw a report on the news this past Saturday about the Sanderson boy. That was what, I think, Mr. Dezmun wanted to talk to me about. Either that case or a similar one."

Keeping his meshed hands on his knee, flexing his fingers in search of the elusive grip, Brinkman glanced up at Poland. "Howard, who's handling the Sanderson case?"

"That's Bayside. Must be Zimmerman," Poland confirmed, arms still akimbo.

"Zimmerman," Brinkman repeated with conviction.

"Zimmerman is very good," Poland added.

Brinkman took the paper with Dezmun's name on it, folded it twice, leaned forward and stuck it into Smith's shirt pocket. As his face loomed nearer, Smith saw that the black dots on his nose and cheeks were not freckles, not spots in the skin but small surface accretions.

"Here's a simple observation," Brinkman said. "Kogat Dezmun is a disturbed individual. Do not take him seriously. Detective Poland and I appreciate your coming to the precinct and offering your cooperation, but let me emphasize that investigating these sorts of things is what we do for a living. It's our profession. We're at it 24/7. We know what we're about." He pointed to Smith's shirt pocket, referring to the folded paper he had just placed there. "Kogat Dezmun? We know all about him. We've heard all his stories. We know what he's up to, and we know what he's done."

"What has he done?" Smith asked.

"Whatever it was, it was a long time ago," Poland replied.

Brinkman concurred. "It didn't add up to much. A little mischief. That's all."

"So!" Poland clapped his hands and gave a nervous smile. "Now that the record's straight, what do we say, case closed?"

"End of story," Brinkman answered. "Howard? Do we have any Cokes?"

"Nope. We're all out."

"I'm not glad to hear that, Howard."

Brinkman started to stand up. Poland had already moved toward the door.

Smith stopped them: "I'm not finished. I haven't told you the most important thing."

"We got work to do," Poland replied. "And it's hot as hell outside."

"And I need a Coke."

"But I haven't told you about the boy in the box."

The detectives traded rapid glances.

Smith took their silence as a signal to continue. "It's Kogat Dezmun's phrase. According to him, there's a boy being kept inside a wooden box. This box may or may not be in the possession of someone Dezmun called the one true beggar. At least that was what I believed he was trying to say."

"You can't be sure," Poland inferred.

"Not about that last point. But I'm virtually certain he said a boy in a box. A naked boy imprisoned in a wooden box: What a terrible, despairing situation to be in!" He felt the detectives knew more than they were letting on. "Could you please tell me what this is all about?"

Brinkman settled back, the clubbiness drained away. His spotted face was deadpan. Poland seemed displeased and began pacing behind Brinkman's chair, loosening his tie and smoothing down his hair.

Smith wished the room had a little clutter; he wished the desk against the wall had been dragged further into the room and made available to him; he wished the lights did not glare so. The fluorescence gave him a headache, and the electricity hummed like the buzzing of an insect.

"Could we go to another room? It's really cold in here, and this light is very harsh."

Poland stopped pacing and glowered. "What kind of game are you trying to play?"

Smith was shocked.

"Aren't our jobs tough enough without you making up stories?"

"I'm not making up stories," Smith retorted, caught off guard by the attack. "I'm trying my best to describe what occurred."

"Don't you think these cases are being handled by experts?"

"Of course I do. That's why I'm here. I know virtually nothing about these cases and have no way of evaluating this person's testimony, and I see it, therefore, as my responsibility to come forward and report what I have witnessed to the appropriately empowered authorities." He looked at each of the detectives to indicate he was referring to them.

"Wonderful," Brinkman cheered with derisive clapping and a big, false smile.

"There are holes in your argument," Poland charged.

"I'm not making an argument," Smith protested.

"Too much hedging." Poland jabbed the air with an index finger. "Too many *I supposes*. Too many *more or lesses*. Maybe Dezmun just told you what he knew you wanted to hear."

Smith shook his head. "I'm just making an honest report."

Poland gripped the back of the empty chair and pounced like a small-eyed owl. "If all this was so important, why did you wait until today before coming to us?"

"He's got a point," Brinkman said.

"I should have done that immediately," Smith admitted. "I made a mistake. I didn't realize at first the seriousness of the situation. I should have contacted you right after the second encounter, or at the latest once I learned he had followed me to the park."

"Why were you at the park?" Poland asked.

"It was a nice day," Smith answered the needlessly contentious question. "What difference does it make why I was there?"

"Maybe Dezmun was there for the same reason," Brinkman suggested. "It was a nice day. Maybe he felt *you* followed *him*."

"No, he followed me. Not only that, but his family sits day and night in the window that overlooks the entrance to the building and watches everybody go in and out."

"How do you know?" Poland asked.

"I see them," he answered obviously. "I see them when I go in, and I see them when I go out. I can see them in their window when I look down from my own kitchen window."

"Then who's observing whom?" Brinkman wondered. "Perhaps the truth is that you have been observing them far more than they have been observing you."

"We see paranoids all the time," Poland said. "They think everybody's watching them." He mimicked: "'People are talking about me! People are following me!' Relax! Nobody's following you."

Brinkman concurred. "Even if you think you understood what our friend, Mr. Dezmun, said to you, what you took away from your discussion was most likely an inaccurate translation. You see, you had to fill in the gaps in order to make sense of what he was trying to tell you. For example, when Mr. Dezmun told you these things, about this boy and so forth, did he use the word 'imprisoned' as you just did when you told us? I ask that because 'imprisoned' does not sound like an item in Mr. Dezmun's verbal repertoire."

"He babbles," Smith acknowledged. "His English is very bad."

"Well then, if it's unlikely that Mr. Dezmun used the word 'imprisoned', why did you use it in your presentation just now?"

Smith shrugged. Brinkman's point was valid but puny. "If there is a boy inside a box, it's possible, if not probable, he's there against his will."

"Did he use the word 'naked'?" Poland asked, adopting the new tactic.

"Yes, I believe he did," Smith answered. "And I'm certain he said a wooden box. But these details don't really matter."

"Oh, but they do," Brinkman insisted with a patronizing smile. "These details matter most of all." His smile expanded. He spread his arms to take control. "Details like these break cases wide open."

Smith hugged himself. "Could we go into the Complaint Room? It was warmer in there."

Brinkman showed his hands: It was only air, he seemed to say. There was nothing he could do.

"Then can you at least open the door?"

Brinkman's telephone rang. He excused himself, pulled the phone out of its sheath, pressed a button and held it to his ear: "Brinkman here . . . That's exactly what I've been saying . . . Yes . . . Good enough." He pressed a button to end the call and resheathed the phone. "That was him," he said to Poland, then smiled at Smith. "Sorry about that." He reclasped his knee, flexing his fingers. "Now, where were we?"

"We were saying how we've got everything under control," Poland answered. "And how this Dezmun character is insane."

"Oh, yes," Brinkman confirmed. "Crazy Mr. Dezmun."

Finally sitting down on the available chair, Poland leaned forward to complete the triangle of heads and, in all seriousness, declared: "I don't even think that guy's human. Have you seen his teeth?" he asked Smith. "They're not human teeth."

Brinkman rolled his eyes. "He's an extremely ugly man, Howard. Let's just leave it at that."

"So don't play games with him," Poland warned.

"I don't play games with him."

"Don't even talk to him," Brinkman advised. "Don't listen to him."

"Don't do anything," Poland stressed. "Do absolutely nothing."

"Well, not 'absolutely' nothing," Brinkman corrected.

Poland defended himself. "I didn't mean 'absolutely' nothing."

"We know you didn't mean 'absolutely' nothing, Howard. Now let's go get some Cokes."

The detectives stood up. Brinkman turned to Smith in an attempt to sum up. "Go home. Go to the movies. Go to the beach. Do whatever it is you do when you're not thinking about the crazy foreigner who cleans your hallways."

Smith stayed seated. "Is that all you're going to do?"

Brinkman shrugged. "What more do you want us to do?"

"Aren't you going to at least write something down?"

"That's not necessary," Brinkman said.

"That means paperwork," Poland explained. "They kill us here with paperwork."

Smith was incredulous. "Shouldn't you file a report?"

"A report about what?" Poland asked.

"About the boy in the box."

Poland and Brinkman sighed and shook their heads. They exchanged glances, as if confirming their entente and a shared frustration. Each sat back down at the points of the triangle. Brinkman again crossed his legs and gripped his knee. Poland further loosened his tie, the knot of which now reached his chest.

"Mr. Smith, we can talk to you all day if you'd like," Brinkman said.

"We don't want to go back to work." Poland giggled and eyed the closed door. "We still get paid."

"Howard, if we're going to sit here for a while, I have to have a Coke."

Poland shrugged. "I already told you: There are no more."

"I'm not glad to hear that, Howard. I'm not at all glad to hear that."

Smith was seized by a sinking feeling. He had hoped to shift his burden to the shoulders of professionals but instead was facing a pair poorly equipped and insufficiently sturdy—a pair too jaded and arrogant, a pair convinced, foolishly, that only they could ask the right questions.

He looked at each man's face: subtle, mottled, nervous, beaked. Smith could see that each had information and that each was prepared to conceal what he knew.

"What about the one true beggar?" Smith asked. "As I told you, Dezmun mentioned him. Who is he?"

"Exactly where did our friend Mr. Dezmun say we might find this so-called beggar?" Brinkman asked.

"He didn't say. At least not so that I understood. He did mention Chinatown."

"Stay away from Chinatown," Poland cautioned, standing up and stepping back behind the chair. "There's nothing there but rats."

"And greasy food."

"They put rats in the food. That's all they eat over there."

Smith ignored the commentary. "He also said the boy was 'outside' in some sense. Inside the box, but outside of something else. Inside, outside. He uses those words a lot. Maybe because he pronounces them well. They may not even have the same meanings for him as they do for us."

Poland smirked. "Again, too much hedging." He raised his voice and thrust demonstratively with his finger. "Too many *mights* and *maybes* and *possiblys* and *could bes* and *I don't knows*. We don't operate like that."

"Don't forget the miming and gestures," Brinkman added.

Poland threw up his hands and lamented. "Like we work in a zoo! Like we're supposed to know what it means when a monkey hoots and pounds his chest or picks his butt!"

"Please." Brinkman held up a hand to slow his colleague's agitation. "Monkeys don't pound their chests. Gorillas pound their chests. Monkeys swing from trees. Howard, you should know that."

For an instant, Poland froze, then let go a spiteful laugh. He started grunting, pounding his chest like an ape, scratching his sides, hopping from one foot to the other.

Brinkman chuckled without making a sound, but the flab of his torso heaved up and down. "Let's not forget the beggar."

Poland launched a pantomime by bending over and hobbling around the room, displaying a beggar's outstretched hand.

Brinkman howled with laughter. "Howard, what are you doing?" he asked, his laugh subsiding. "That's not the one true beggar. That's the one true gimp." He wiped away a ludicrous tear. "He does a great gimp," he confided to Smith. "You do a great gimp," he told Poland.

Smith had to take the silly boys in hand. He blurted out, cool and clear: "What about the boy in the box?"

The giggles weakened and dissipated; serious, thoughtful demeanors returned.

"You said the boy was naked, is that right?" Brinkman inquired.

"Not I. Kogat Dezmun said the boy was naked."

"Granted. Now let's assume for a moment that there is a naked boy. How naked is he?"

"What do you mean?"

"How naked?" Poland asked, following his partner's lead. "Just exactly how naked is naked?"

The detectives were poised, leaning forward, hands on knees, awaiting Smith's explanation.

"Naked is naked!" Smith did not know what else to say. "A person can't be partially naked."

"Why not?" Poland asked. "A person can be completely naked. When you take off all your clothes, aren't you then completely naked?"

"Is naked the same as nude?" Brinkman inquired with a scholarly air. "Can a person be nude and not be naked?"

Breathing hard through his gaping mouth, Poland peered at Smith. "Have you ever been completely naked?"

"What if I have a ring on my finger and nothing else?" Brinkman wondered. "Am I naked, or am I only nude?"

Smith repeated what was, for him, the only meaningful question: "What about the boy in the box?"

Brinkman rolled his eyes. Poland sighed and ran both hands over his scalp. Brinkman inched to the edge of his chair and took a deep breath. "Listen to me," he urged Smith, his voice subdued. "I insist that you believe what it is I am about to say because I may say it only once." He cleared his throat and rubbed his hands. "There is no boy," he declared. "There is no box. They don't exist. They aren't real."

"I know what it is," Poland said, smugly shaking a finger at Smith. "You've been watching too much TV."

"I don't believe that's it, Howard. I believe our friend Mr. Smith is one of those who thinks too much."

Smith objected: "It's not possible to think too much."

Brinkman smiled. "You just proved my point."

Smith's patience had run out. He leaped up, clenched his fists, raised his voice: "Stop this nonsense!"

The detectives looked startled. Brinkman dropped his hands to his sides and tipped the chair back on its legs. Poland had stopped in midstride with his body half-turned.

"There may be a boy in a box," Smith began, "or there may not be a boy in a box. Either way, children are being reported missing, and then this man comes along, conveys to me details of a kidnapping, and you two find it laughable."

The detectives waited.

"First you behave like impatient clerks, then like a pair of clowns. I had assumed that the authorities took reports of missing children seriously and conducted thorough investigations. It seems to me that the only investigation under way in this precinct is into making crude jokes and shirking duty." Smith was shivering. The frigid room felt deeper than a basement, more buried, like a vault. "Now it is unhealthily cold in here," he stated. "If we are to remain in this room, I insist that the air-conditioning be turned down."

Brinkman became pensive as if considering the demand. He looked up at Poland, who shrugged.

"Mr. Smith," Brinkman began, "you are an industrial designer. What exactly is it that you design?"

Smith detected an unctuous tone but answered nevertheless. "Consumer products."

"Such as?"

"Well, for example, I've been revamping a dustpan."

Brinkman's spotted face bloomed with a delighted smile. Poland, meanwhile, stared slack-jawed in disbelief. "You revamp dustpans?" he asked.

"That's just an example."

"You're telling us that you barge in here, you take up our time, you insult us, and you revamp dustpans?"

"Now, Howard, he meant no offense."

Poland jabbed a finger at Smith's face. "Listen up, you shit shoveler: Before you revamp your next dustpan, you'd better revamp yourself." The detective stepped back and brushed down his hair.

"Perhaps I should tell my story to the media," Smith suggested weakly. "They'll know what to do with it."

"Do you think they're going to listen to you?" Poland sneered. "What do you think, they don't have a hundred stupid stories like this one? And you're going to go there and say there 'might be' a missing boy. Yeah, there might be a missing chicken, there might be a missing Rolls Royce, there might be a missing banana."

"Howard, let's be civil," Brinkman cautioned.

"This guy thinks he's the only decent person on the planet," Poland said.

"Howard, please calm down." Brinkman looked at Smith. "What's your first name?"

Smith hesitated, mistrustful of the detective's attempt to soften the confrontation. "Perhaps," he replied, "for the moment at least, we should stick with last names."

This remark hit Brinkman hard, as if a line had been crossed, a gauntlet hurled down. Brinkman was not to be bullied. He tightened his lips, breathed deeply, pressed down on his thighs, pushed up his bulk, lifting his rotund self off the chair, and, once on his feet, staggered forward and glared indignantly. "Just who in the hell do you think you are talking to, *Mr.* Smith?"

Poland stepped in but not to cool things down. "What kind of a name is Smith anyway? It's a name for a perp. It's a name a perp uses when he doesn't want to give his real name. 'Mr. Smith, Mr. Jones, Mr. John Q. Public.'"

"Smith is my real name."

"Understand something, *Mr.* Smith!" Brinkman bellowed, mocking the formality of the title. He loomed so close Smith smelled cologne and could count the accretions on the perforated skin. "You don't know diddly-squat, *Mr.* Smith! You don't need to know diddly-squat."

Smith was stung by the nasty turn. "You're trying to confuse me," he countered, grasping for a last line of reason. "Bad cop, bad cop. What happened to good cop, bad cop?"

"Good cop, bad cop?" Poland echoed.

Brinkman improvised: "Black cop, white cop? Or would you prefer coffee-colored?"

"Fat cop, skinny cop," Poland continued, cocking his head at the sound of the words like a bird keying in.

"*Mr.* Smith!" Brinkman had regained his phony affability but still derided Smith's name. "You're not trying to set up our friend *Mr.* Dezmun, are you?"

"Of course not!"

"Maybe you're trying to get back at that old man for some reason," Poland suggested. "Maybe because he looked at you the wrong way."

"Or maybe because he threw you a kiss. You did say he was in love with you."

"Maybe you're in love with him. And you're jealous because of his wife."

"This is outrageous!" Smith's outcry convinced no one. He was shaking from the cold and the agitation.

Brinkman clarified. "It's not unusual for a man to commit a crime and then return to the scene or visit the police and offer information implicating some innocent person. That's how we catch a good number of our suspects."

"I'd say at least half."

"They do a crime, then march into this very room, sit us down in these very chairs and try to dump the blame on somebody else."

Smith's voice shook with umbrage. "What are you insinuating?"

"Just that you're a shit shoveler," Poland shot back. "What do you think?" he asked Brinkman. "Have we got ourselves a shit shoveler or something even sicker?"

"Howard, I think we've caught ourselves a kidnapper."

"A boy stealer!" Poland smiled, and his eyes shone, excited for the first time.

Brinkman speculated. "Or maybe he's the boy stolen."

"Yes." Poland drew a conclusion. "He's the boy in the box."

Smith groaned, which was all he could do.

"That's what our friend Mr. Dezmun called you, isn't that so?" Poland asked. "His alabaster boy?"

"No!"

Poland pushed his face close to Smith's and leered. "So you're his little naked alabaster boy," he whispered.

"Stop it!"

Poland's eyes sparkled. "Was this little boy castrated? Is that how Kogat Dezmun likes his little boys?" He ran his tongue along his lips as if he, too, liked his boys that way.

Brinkman intervened, also coming closer. Smith now stood between the two imposing faces.

"What my partner is getting at," Brinkman explained, "is that if there really were a boy in a box, he would have to be castrated. Otherwise, how would he fit? Which makes me wonder, *Mr.* Smith, being castrated and all, when you stand up, do you feel the wind blowing between your legs?"

"I want to speak to a lawyer."

The detectives exploded in laughter. Brinkman squealed and held his sides. Poland hopped up and down, provoked by the hilarity. To Smith, they more than ever mimicked chimpanzees.

"Shut up!" Smith shouted. "You're both idiots!"

Poland thrust his fierce face right up to Smith's and screamed: "There is no boy in the box!"

Smith screamed back: "I don't know that!"

Poland grabbed Smith by the shirt and hurled him against the concrete wall, banging the back of Smith's head at the line where the two blues met. Smith slumped to the floor, dizzy, stupefied, steeped in cobalt, squinting up into glaring fluorescence, ensnared by the insect hum.

Over him hovered Poland scowling, growling like a bear. Despite the coolness, a bead of sweat hung from the barbed end of the detective's nose. With his mouth wide open, Poland reached down to inflict more damage.

"Okay, cool it." Brinkman's command halted the assault.

Poland straightened up, smoothed down his hair, buttoned his collar and with three quick definitive jerks, tightened his tie, once and for all.

The fat detective bent down, propped himself up on one knee and addressed the humbled citizen. "Mr. Smith, you came here today as if you were going to save the world. I believe you're well intentioned but misdirected. Now, so far, there's been no real harm done, so why don't you go home, live your life, forget about these crazy rumors. Let us do our job. We're the professionals."

"In other words," Poland clarified, "don't waste our time."

"If you meddle, you'll get in the way. If we need you, we'll call on you. We have your phone number."

"No, we don't," Poland said.

"Well, then Mr. Smith will write it down for us. In the meantime," Brinkman addressed Smith, "don't be afraid of our friend the janitor."

"The man's a lunatic."

"If we could put him in jail, we would, but there's no crime here."

"If he says anything to you, don't talk back, don't even listen."

"Nothing he says will ever make sense."

"He's a kook, he's a crank."

"He's a crackpot."

"He's a flake."

"He's a bozo."

"He's a schizoid."

"Don't look at him. Don't say hello. Just walk on by. Soon he'll lose interest and start pestering somebody else."

Each of the detectives reached down, took one of Smith's arms, hoisted the dazed, enfeebled man to his feet, dusted him off, straightened his shirt. Then Brinkman put his arm around his shoulders and escorted him into the corridor.

"We don't have an easy job here," Brinkman confessed, his voice weary and consoling. "But somebody's got to do it."

"We can't all revamp dustpans," Poland needled jocularly.

They walked Smith to the front entrance. "Go home, Mr. Smith," Brinkman advised. He shook Smith's hand. "Get some sleep."

Smith wrote down his phone number on a pad that Poland brought him. Then Poland shook his hand.

"Come on, Howard," Brinkman said. "Let's go get some Cokes."

TEN

Outside the precinct station the sky was haze, and almost immediately Smith began to sweat. Compared with the iciness of the Community Room, the sticky air was pleasant, but by the time he walked a block and crossed a congested street, his temples throbbed and his breathing had grown labored.

Adopting a stony frown and realizing how hungry he had become, he marched into Wendy's coffee shop. A lunchtime crowd was buzzing. All the booths were occupied. Wendy was busy and unable to talk. He took a stool at the counter, next to an elderly woman who sipped coffee from a cup she held in both hands. She wore a black dress and a pillbox hat with a lace veil turned up on the brim. Her face was heavily powdered, and her mouth gleamed with ruby-red lipstick. By her elbow lay a muffin, partially eaten, like a crumbling ruin.

Down onto the last available stool plopped a brawny construction worker wearing tattoos, work jeans, work boots, a five o'clock shadow. He had come in after Smith and yelled his order, calling the waiter "Joe." The harried Joe, whom Smith had not seen working there before, had just rushed out to service a booth and responded to the call by hurrying back behind the counter and providing the loud customer a napkin, knife and fork.

"Hey!" Smith shouted. "Joe! That's not fair! I was here first!"

The diners at the counter, clutching cups or utensils, stopped eating and looked at Smith.

"I want eggs, Joe!" Smith barked. He had gotten Joe's attention. Others in the restaurant took note. Smith glanced at Wendy and saw that she, too, was watching.

"Scrambled eggs!" Smith shouted. "On the double!"

Joe nodded and turned toward the kitchen.

"And a napkin, knife and fork! Just like everybody else!"

Joe hastened back to Smith with a napkin, knife and fork, then poured Smith a glass of water.

"Coffee!" Smith ordered. "Why would I want water?"

Dishes had come out from the kitchen and sat steaming on the counter. Joe took two or three in each arm.

"Where's that coffee?" Smith called peevishly.

"One moment," Joe pleaded. He was pale and frail. His hair was thin and combed straight back. His hands gripped the dishes securely, with experience and confidence; they had long, strong fingers and enlarged veins that raised the skin, like the roots of a tree. Having taken a second to catch his breath, he rushed toward the booths to deliver the food.

"Relax, pal," the construction worker called to Smith from down the counter. "There's enough coffee for everybody."

For an instant he and Smith locked stares. The worker's face was blunt and blocky and the gaze unflinching. To show that he accepted the man's comment without hard feelings, Smith raised his water in a salute, and the worker responded, lifting his fork.

The eggs came, and with a smile Smith thanked the waiter, apologizing for his impatience though noting how his loud, obtrusive style had gotten him what he wanted.

He turned to the elderly woman in the pillbox hat. She was staring ahead, as if lost in a thought. Smith tried, in his mind, to penetrate the layers of her privacy. He scraped off her indifference and her self-containment, removed the hot dress and the pasty cosmetics, pared her down to the pit: the bare skin, the guarded thought. Beyond that point, was there more to take off?

"Excuse me," he said. "May I ask you something?"

The woman did not hear him, or else she pretended she did not.

Smith asked his question nevertheless: "Do you know anything about a boy in a box?"

With sagging bags under sad, gray eyes, the woman looked at Smith, saying nothing, but the knowledgeable gaze showed him that she had heard and had understood what he had asked, that she could have answered had she chosen to, that she knew the answer. She had seen it, her look conveyed; she had put her gnarled hands around it; she had tasted it; she had raised the steaming magic to her lips and sipped.

ELEVEN

A boy in a box? How could a boy fit in a box?

A one true beggar? The city was overrun by beggars: filthy beggars, articulate beggars, beggars who wore overcoats in summer, beggars who shouted down phantoms and danced furious protestations, beggars who stood stock still for hours, beggars who stole young boys and locked them in small wooden boxes.

Would his story be sensational enough for the newspapers and television? The detectives were probably right: Journalists had heard thousands of stories like his, had broadcast hundreds of stories far more frightening and obscene; stories made of facts, with photographs and witnesses. All he had was a nightmare and the lurid babble of a dirty old man. Publicizing his story would only subject him to ridicule and deeper suspicion.

Deeper suspicion. The phrase echoed as if he had heard it before. His thinking was cluttered with borrowed phrases.

After thirty minutes in the subway headed toward downtown Manhattan, Smith became restless and got off sooner than planned. On Broadway, he walked as the others did: rapid, determined, detached. His eye caught a passing glance, which may have collided with his accidentally or may have selected him from out of the crowd, on purpose, with forethought.

He stopped dead and spun around to see who might be following. No one reacted except for a man who frowned at Smith for halting so abruptly and causing him to break his stride.

Smith stopped a woman in a chiffon dress.

"Excuse me. How far is Chinatown?"

"Chinatown? That's rather far from here."

"Can I walk?"

"Oh, dear!" She knit her brow. Her lips were the color of shells. Her hair was white like a clean cloud. "I would recommend the subway. Or a taxi."

"Excuse me." He stopped her from walking off. "Have you ever heard of the one true beggar?"

Her face slammed shut, and she hurried on her way.

Smith stepped to the curb and raised his hand. Soon a yellow taxi pulled up in front of him.

He settled into the backseat.

"Chinatown."

The driver penciled a note on a clipboard, started the meter and veered into traffic. The man had dark hair and thick hands. Beneath the meter, attached to the license, hung his photograph and his name: Mohammed Mohedi.

At the first red light, Smith leaned forward and spoke through the partition. "Excuse me."

Mohedi tilted his head toward the sound of Smith's voice.

"Do you know someone called the one true beggar?"

Mohedi glanced at Smith in the rearview mirror.

"The one true beggar?" Smith repeated.

Mohedi glanced quickly over his shoulder. "No, sir."

Just as Smith readied a second and more important question, the light changed, the cab surged forward, and he was thrown back against the seat. He closed his eyes against the fleeting hurly-burly of the streets, gasping with relief when they reached their destination.

Mott Street was crammed with shoppers, mostly Chinese, among whom Smith dodged and shifted. The markets were bursting with robust vegetables and bins of diverse foods: dehydrated shrimp, peanuts, gingerroots, bean sprouts, garlic cloves, dusty-colored mushrooms wrinkled like shrunken ears.

From a truck, workers were unloading spinach packed in wooden crates and stacking the crates on hand trucks. The boxes were knee-high, made of plywood, fastened with nails and bound with wire. The slats were spaced an inch apart, granting a wide enough opening for a tiny prisoner to peer out, glimpse patches of the world and watch how it worked.

All around him swirled the Chinese language, an inexhaustible singsong floating and lilting among the clerks and the customers, inside and outside the shops. Signs and awnings bellowed stark, vivid Chinese characters in yellow, orange, red, conveying messages Smith could study forever and never understand.

For sale were plastic toys, wooden back-scratchers, jeweled China eggs, statuettes of turtles and Buddhas, tea sets, fans, parasols.

A fish market displayed tubs of water with live eels and helpless lobsters whose claws were bound by yellow bands. Whole fish arranged on ice shimmered under lamps. Smith identified flounder, sardines, shrimp, squid. A red-pink, scintillating fish, still asphyxiating, flapped its gills and stared from a hapless eye.

Inside the market, workers in blood-stained smocks and rubber gloves were weighing fish in hanging scales. They removed the heads and fins with scissors, gutted and rinsed the bellies, passed the fish to an older woman who wrapped them first in wax paper, then in plastic bags.

Smith was nauseated by the stench and the slimy floors. He approached the woman wrapping the fish. Her face was round like a wafer and grooved like the bark of a tree.

"Excuse me. I'm looking for the one true beggar. Do you know him?"

The woman did not understand. She looked at the cashier behind the register, a glum teenage girl with pimply cheeks.

"Mister?" the girl's soft voice piped. "Can I help you?"

"Yes, I'm looking for a man called the one true beggar."

"Sorry?"

Smith restated slowly. "The one true beggar."

"Sorry?" She looked lost.

"He may be a peddler."

The girl shook her head.

"He may have a box with him. A wooden box. Something like those." He pointed at discarded crates stacked up by the back door.

The young girl grimaced. The old woman barked in Chinese, and in response one of the cleaners emerged from behind the counter. His smock was drenched and spattered. He had small eyes and a pit in the middle of his forehead. A gloved hand gripped the gutting knife.

"What you want?" the worker asked.

"The boy in the box."

"We no have."

"Who has?"

"We no have."

"Who has?" Smith shouted. "Who? Who? Who?"

The man glowered but stood his ground. In the shop, all movement ceased.

Smith stepped back, away from the contaminated smock.

The old and worried woman uttered more Chinese.

The shoppers and workers, seized by the tension, watched anxiously. No one spoke or moved or shifted their eyes from the angry man standing in the middle of the shop.

"I'm just trying to behave properly!" Smith declared, almost pleadingly. "Why is that so astounding?" He scanned the unsmiling faces. "There's a boy in a box! Doesn't anybody care?"

No one responded. The Chinese held their breath. Smith balled his fists, then stamped his way out of the shop.

TWELVE

Turning west on Bayard Street, he found, at the end of the block, a park with benches, a dilapidated pavilion and a ball field made of asphalt. The park was crowded. Every bench was occupied, mostly by old men and women with exhausted faces. They sat in the heat, fanning themselves or mopping their brows with handkerchiefs, staring ahead like wrinkled toads at nothing in particular.

Card players sat around a table while a Latin man on a bicycle hovered behind them watching the game. Two tourists, a couple equipped with a camera, backpack and guidebook, were examining a map. Squirrels rustled in the bushes and birds whistled strengthlessly, weakened as well, it seemed, by the sultriness.

Smith traversed a small plaza to the opposite side of the park. Across the street was the Criminal Courts building.

Men and women hurried in and out of the tall bronze doors. From where he stood, he could read the inscription carved in granite on the lintel: "Justice is the firm and continuous Desire to Render to Everyman his Due."

He sat down at the end of a bench, next to two Chinese men. With his hand he wiped the sweat from his neck and brow and could feel through his shirt the wetness under his arms and down his back. The Chinese men next to him were smoking cigarettes. Each was elderly and displayed a rugged, weary face. Not far off a homeless man rifled through a trash barrel, dropping the retrieved bottles and cans into a plastic garbage bag. Farther down the path, on the Chinatown side, against the wrought-iron fence that enclosed a children's playground, two men, one white, one black, huddled in conversation.

Smith stood up and approached the homeless man scavenging through the trash. He came up from behind, then, thinking better of it, circled around to his front, granting the stranger adequate space.

The man was bent over with his head and arms inside the barrel. Black flies danced on the rim.

"Excuse me."

At the sound of Smith's voice, the flies scattered. The man jerked up, his eyes paranoid. He wore a tattered shirt and smelled like trash.

"Sorry for disturbing you. I was just wondering if, by any chance, you knew someone referred to as the one true beggar?"

The man stared, uncomprehending.

"The one true beggar. Might you be he?" Smith asked. The man stared.

"Do you know anything about a boy in a box?"

"I don't know nobody like that. Next door, maybe." With that terse reply, he stuck his head back down into the barrel and resumed rummaging.

One of the individuals huddling by the playground gate broke away and started toward Smith. He was a wiry black man wearing dungarees and a yellow T-shirt.

"What you want?" he called to Smith as they came face-to-face. His skin glistened with perspiration. "What you looking for?" With fingers spread, he thrust his hands down, indicating the ground between his feet as if something lay buried there. He took nervous steps back and forth, glanced furtively around the park, checked the passersby, looked back once at his companion, who was watching from the playground gate. He pointed to himself: "Walter." He smiled, revealing a missing bottom tooth.

Smith felt uncomfortable giving up his name. "I'd rather not identify myself just yet."

"Fuck you, man! Don't play games with me!"

Walter was thinner and shorter than Smith, and, despite his posture and his words, conveyed a minimal threat.

"You came here, man, because you want something. So tell me what you want."

"I want the boy in the box."

A jolting excitation seized Walter's body. He moaned and shivered, then spun around on his left leg as if twirling in a manic dance. "Oh, man!" he blurted out, coming to a halt. He glanced back at his companion who was observing intently from outside the playground.

A passerby approached, a woman heading for the courts, and Walter dipped his head and stared at his feet until she was out of earshot. He then got down to business. "I tell you what, man. You give me fifty dollars, and I get you what you want."

"Do you have what I want?"

"I can get it." Walter kept his voice low and under control. "You want this bad. Anybody can see that, and I can bring it right here." Again he gestured to the paving stone between his feet. "But first you got to give me fifty bucks. The man don't give away shit for free."

"Is 'the man' the one true beggar?"

"The man is the man." Walter came closer. His eyes were bloodshot and edgy, his breath shallow and quick. He was unshaven, with white bristles carpeting his sunken cheeks and running the length of his jaw. His collarbone was pronounced. His bronze skin gave off a sweaty, polished glow. "The man got what you want."

"And what is that?" Smith asked skeptically. "What is it that I want? I don't think you know."

Walter groaned. "Don't be an asshole, man! This is reality. Right now you ain't got shit. You got a dream. That's all you got. Give me the money and I make the motherfucker real."

"First get it. First show it to me. Then we'll discuss compensation."

"Don't be an asshole, man. I need the money up front."

A park worker was raking leaves. A young woman was pulling at the leashes of two large dogs. Along the street cruised a police car, which Smith hardly noticed, but Walter spotted it right away and stood still until it passed.

"Okay, man, let's work this out. Forty-five dollars. That's the best I can do."

Smith did not trust him. "I wish to speak to the one true beggar."

"Say what?"

"I wish to speak to the one true beggar. Are you he?"

"Am I who?"

"The one true beggar."

Walter cringed, balled his fists, spun around, took a few steps, cursed to himself, cursed at the trees, then strutted back to Smith. Sweat clung to the tip of Walter's nose and beaded on his short-cropped hair. His voice was low and controlled: "I know that dude," he whispered.

"Are you he?"

"No, I ain't he. What's wrong with you?"

"Bring him to me," Smith demanded. "No money up front. Otherwise, I'm leaving."

"Oh, man!" Walter shook his head at Smith's contentiousness. Then he stiffened, calm and cool, no panic, no ecstasy. "Wait right here. Don't go nowhere."

He headed toward the playground and waved for his partner to meet him halfway. They conferred in the middle of the path. Walter shaped an explanation with his agitated hands, bounding up onto the balls of his feet, tiptoeing back and forth. The friend listened. Walter kept on talking and gesticulating until the two turned simultaneously and hurried, side by side, soberly and urgently, back to where Smith stood waiting.

Despite the sultry heat, the friend had on a plaid flannel shirt with the sleeves rolled down to the wrists and the collar button closed, and he still looked cold. His unsmiling face was pale and spectral. He stepped forward, gaunt and glaring. Walter stood behind him like an athlete warming up, bouncing on his tiptoes, as if prepared to leap forward or run away.

"What's your name?" Smith asked the newcomer.

"Never mind my name." His manner was clipped and hostile.

Smith shrugged. In his mind, the man already had a name: Smith would call him Bones.

"Are you a team?" Smith asked.

"What if we are?" Bones answered.

"Are you the one true beggar?"

"What if I am?"

Walter was impatient. "Tell the man here what you want."

Smith looked at Bones. "I want the boy in the box."

Walter stopped fidgeting. Bones was cold, but the intensity in his eyes showed that he was listening.

Smith repeated his request, enunciating slowly. "The boy in the box."

Bones nodded to Walter, who flashed his broken smile. "Man, I told you. This is reality. You want dreams, you go elsewhere. But if you want reality, you got it right here." Once more, he pointed at the ground.

"Fifty bucks," Bones demanded.

"Fifty dollars is too much," Smith countered. "Walter has already come down to forty-five."

"Fifty bucks, man! Now that ain't shit." Walter again sought to temper his tone. "We can get you what you want, man, but we got to go to work. You hear what I'm saying? We got to break the rules."

"What rules?"

"The rules! The rules! The motherfucking rules!" Walter stomped the ground and pressed his hands between his thighs, then, by way of explanation, opened his arms to indicate the park and all that was surrounding it. "What do you think makes this shit work?"

"I'm sorry," Smith said. "But I don't believe you know what I'm looking for."

Bones responded, "The boy in the box."

The words had come quickly, with no hesitation, chillingly direct, as pale and as cool as the skull that had uttered them. Smith imagined Bones as a man who lived in a basement and rarely saw the sun, who hardly ate, who seldom slept, whose blood was ice and, judging from the dryness of his skin in such sweltering heat, who abstained from ingesting adequate fluids.

But he had uttered the phrase, *the boy in the box*. For the first time Smith heard the words intoned in just the way he had always pronounced them to himself. And they echoed now, making a connection, pointing in a direction, possibly a solution.

Bones stepped forward, boring in. "You want us to break the rules? You make it worth our while. How much you got?"

Smith stood frozen.

"We got to know this, man. How much you got?"

Smith took out his wallet. The billfold contained more than a hundred dollars.

Walter and Bones leaned and leered: a wedded pair of compulsive faces.

A troop of sailors in white uniforms had entered the park and were crossing the asphalt ball field. They were young and excited and concerned only with themselves. Nor were the wizened Chinese smokers paying attention to Smith's negotiations.

"Twenty dollars," Smith offered.

Walter's knees buckled. He clawed his neck.

"You got to do better than that." Bones glared. "What the fuck do you do?"

"I'm an industrial designer."

Bones was incredulous. "A designer? You got designs?"

"Yes, I do."

Bones looked at Walter. "The asshole's got designs."

Walter started laughing. It was a rough, irregular laugh, almost like a cough.

"Let's see some fucking cash." Bones demanded. "Fifty dollars, that's as low as we go."

"Thirty dollars," Smith countered.

Bones stabbed a finger at Smith's face. His teeth were clenched, his mouth having narrowed to a cold, hissing hole: "Fifty dollars, you fucking asshole! Take it or leave it."

"Take it or leave it, man. You can't do both. You take the motherfucker or you leave it. If you want a boy bad,

I mean, if you want him so bad you can almost taste him, man, you got to give something up. You hear what I'm saying? Do you hear what I am saying?"

Bones and Walter would not budge, or at least Smith did not know how to make them move. Further haggling might scuttle the chance. He withdrew three twenty-dollar bills from his wallet.

"Do you have change?" he asked.

Walter raged: "Man! Look at us! We ain't got no change! Do we look like we got change? Now, just give my man here what you got. Enough of this bullshit!"

Smith hesitated. "I get ten dollars' change. A deal's a deal."

"A deal ain't no deal, you asshole, until you give us the fucking money." Bones's ferocious eyes had clamped onto the bills clenched in Smith's fist, already claiming them.

Walter stepped up, suddenly calm and conciliatory. "Listen, my man." He strained to sound trustful and confidential. "You got to help us out. We got to work together. I mean, how much do you need this boy? I mean, how much do you love him?"

"Now that's the fucking question."

The desperate, strung-out faces awaited Smith's reply.

"I don't exactly know him," Smith answered, "but I can honestly say I love him enough to want to set him free."

"Then let's do it, man. Make it real."

They would not settle for less. Smith had to chance it; either that or walk away.

"I expect the merchandise in full and ten dollars' change when this is over."

In a single motion, Bones snatched the money and whirled. The two partners hurried back to the playground, where they waited for Smith to catch up.

"Wait in there," Bones said, pointing inside the iron fence.

The playground was filled with children. It contained mazelike jungle gyms built of wooden beams, blocks and crossbars, over and through which children clambered and played tag. As the mothers and grandmothers looked on from shaded benches at the perimeter, the children, undaunted by the heat, squealed, jumped, danced under sprinklers, dangled from monkey bars, skated down sliding ponds, rocked on swings like pendulums, oblivious to who was watching just outside their gated grounds.

"I'm not waiting in there," Smith objected.

"Are you scared of kids?" challenged Bones.

Smith did not answer.

"The asshole's scared of kids," Bones concluded.

"Forget the asshole," Walter said.

Bones agreed. The pair turned, went up the path and out of the park.

Smith followed.

They headed down a narrow street named Mosco. In the middle of the block a Chinese restaurant and a tenement were separated by an alleyway blocked by trash cans and closed with an iron picket gate, painted brown, scrolled at the bottom, topped by spear points. Behind it the alley ran twenty feet to a brick wall, above which a barbed wire fence guarded a courtyard where linens were flapping on laundry lines.

Bones did not hesitate. He gripped the top of the gate, just below the spikes, vaulted up, set his right foot on the top rail, shifted his grip, swung his left leg over, then brought his right leg down, lowering himself to the ground on the other side. Immediately he turned and ran toward the wall.

Walter confronted Smith. "Listen to me, man." He was furious and menacing. "You stay here. Don't follow us. You hear what I'm saying?"

Smith saw that a boundary had been reached; pushing further could do him harm.

"How long will you be?"

"Ten minutes, man. That's all we need."

Smith watched as Walter vaulted the gate as nimbly as Bones had done and, once down, raced after his friend who had already scaled the rear wall, negotiated the barbed wire and disappeared beneath the flapping sheets. Walter followed, vanishing without looking back.

Smith faced the sloping street. To the west was the park and the courts. Looking east, where the block-long Mosco ended at Mott Street, he saw the interminable shopping stream. A brick church with Gothic windows occupied the corner, not far from the Bangkok Grocery, whose green awning bore squiggly words in a yellow alphabet. Above the awning, fire escapes ascended the sides of the building like scales or rusted skin. The tenements possessed brick bodies, curtained eyes, and wrought-iron hands tipped by spear points.

Thick gray clouds had rolled in to darken the sky and raise the humidity. The overfull air was about to burst; it had to burst; it could not stop from bursting.

Ten minutes passed. Pedestrians hurried by and kept their heads down.

It thundered. Twenty minutes passed. The clouds had turned nearly black. Smith felt a drop of water and wondered: Had it fallen from a cloud or from an air conditioner in an upstairs window?

Thirty minutes passed. Lightning flashed. Real rain arrived in angry, swollen drops. The sky was dark like twilight. He put his hands on his head to keep it dry.

An hour passed. He laughed at himself, not because of the mistakes he had made but because of what he had come to resemble: a rooted beggar laughing at imaginary jokes, by himself, in the rain, waiting for the delivery of his frail and precious cargo.

THIRTEEN

He arrived back in Queens drenched from the thunderstorm, which had lasted almost ninety minutes and splashed down torrentially, cooling the air and turning the streets into spattering streams.

He stopped at the coffee shop and took a stool at the counter. Three stools away sat the fat man across from the mustachioed cashier. Patterns repeated themselves. The same fat man with his jowls and mottled hands, the same cashier, probably the same customers.

He had come not to eat but to speak with Wendy, who soon appeared, seeming tentative, as if recalling Smith's loud behavior during his lunchtime visit earlier that day. She commented on his wet clothes and on how, for a change, he was sitting at the counter.

"I got tired of the same old booth," Smith explained.

"Oh, really?"

"Same old booth, same old eggs, same old life."

"Same old, same old," Wendy echoed. "We're creatures of routine."

"You think so? Even we pioneers?"

She poised her pen and pad. "So, what would you like?" she asked.

"Egg Foo Yung."

She winced. "Wrong restaurant."

"How about a truth sandwich?" He stared into her brown eyes, and she flinched. Abruptly the mood changed.

"I suggest you feast your eyes on the menu." She took the menu from its place between the sugar and napkin dispensers and stood it up in front of him.

He laid it down, explaining in subdued tones that he had not come to eat but to speak privately with her about a serious matter. She looked away uneasily and suggested he wait for the early dinner rush to settle down. In the meantime, she brought him coffee, serviced the diners, made trips to the kitchen, at one point stopping by the cashier for a huddle. The cashier only listened without replying and nodded approval when she was done.

Smith, meanwhile, watched his coffee cool, stirred it with a spoon, gazed up now and then at the sailboats on the emerald sea.

After fifteen minutes, the pace slowed, and Wendy was able to take a break. She slid onto the stool next to his.

"So, what's this all about?" she asked with some impatience.

The fat man was eavesdropping, but he immediately looked away, slipped from the stool and waddled toward the bathroom.

Smith proceeded to relate some of the frustrating experiences of the day. He mentioned the conversation he had had with the police, how steadfastly they had rejected his testimony regarding Kogat Dezmun and the boy in the box. "It's still unclear to me," he said, "whether they disputed the reality of only a particular boy in a particular box or denied the existence of all missing children, boxed or otherwise. Probably they were only trying to humiliate me, simply as a diversion, out of boredom."

Wendy listened apprehensively with her arms crossed, a signal to Smith that he did not have much time.

Hurriedly, he conveyed a confusing description of his interaction with Walter and Bones, needlessly detailing their vulgarity.

A customer signaled for a check.

"I have to go," Wendy said.

"Please." He took her wrist, held it gently and then let go.

She recoiled reproachfully.

"Help me find the boy in the box," he pleaded.

"I don't think so."

She was nervous but steady. Her overbite, now fully restrained, had lost its sexiness. She had become a different person.

"We'll go to Chinatown first, start looking there."

"Why don't you just leave this alone?"

"Because if I find him and he's alive, then I save a life; and if he's dead, well, at least that will prove that he was real and needed to be looked for. That's why I'm asking you: Come with me, Wendy. Please."

"Look," Wendy interjected. "I'm a normal person." Her voice was whispery and joyless. "I'm just a waitress in a coffee shop, trying to be friendly to customers."

"I thought Aries took risks and broke rules," he taunted.

"I was just trying to make conversation."

Smith shook his head to sweep away the delusion: What a disappointment Wendy had turned out to be. Her eyes were cautious and dry, transformed from the playful pair she had displayed during their first meeting.

He leaned forward and lowered his voice. "Your boss there at the register keeps looking at us. Why don't we go somewhere more private? When you're off duty, of course. It'll be easier for me to articulate my thoughts."

Again, the customer signaled for his check.

Wendy moved away, and Smith grabbed her wrist, this time holding it firmly.

"Let go," she snarled.

Smith did not let go. "Help me find the boy."

She gritted her teeth. "I have to get back to work."

He saw that she was lying and squeezed her wrist.

"There may be a boy trapped in a box. Don't you care about that?"

"Let go of me!" She tried to pull away.

"He's suffocating. His bones are broken. His eyes are filled with pus, yet he still looks through the slats. Maybe he sees only lights and shadows. He's probably naked, probably completely naked. And there remains the distinct possibility that he's been castrated as well."

With a startled yelp, she yanked herself free and backed away.

The cashier came out from behind the register, strode up to Smith and ordered him to leave the restaurant. Smith refused but stated how it pleased him that, after so many furtive glances, the man's eyes had finally stepped forward, as it were, and rested squarely and openly on his. The cashier threatened to call the police. Smith laughed. "The police won't do anything," he said. "The police don't even care about a missing child. Why would they worry about a customer who raises his voice in a coffee shop?"

He acknowledged his audience: a dozen diners pausing in their meals, the cook peering from behind the grill, the busboy lugging dishes to the washer, the fat man returning from the john. To these he announced, in a robust and confident voice, that he had committed himself to exposing what they had sought to conceal, namely the atrocious crime that may or may not have taken place. He thrust a finger in the air, emphasizing the decisiveness of what he had to say. "I know all about the boy!" he shouted. "I've known about him from almost the beginning. And, yes, I'll be leaving now. But unlike you," he pointed at the diners and the workers, thrusting with emphasis at Wendy and the cashier, "unlike you and anyone else who might wander into this overpriced, mediocre establishment, I, Smith, will never be back."

FOURTEEN

The humidity had not returned, and the air was significantly cooler. Though it was almost dark, children were still outside playing; an ice cream truck, sounding a jingle, had lured six or seven of them into a line. Smith determined to go directly to the Dezmuns' apartment and engage Kogat Dezmun in a verbal face-to-face, as prolonged a sit-down as was necessary, with paper and pencil, maps and dictionaries, interpreters if need be, and, once and for all, make some sense of the nagging affair. As the entrance to the building came into view, he accelerated the plan. The figure in the first-floor window was still too distant to be discerned perfectly, but the mop of hair was unmistakable: Kogat Dezmun was leaning out over the sill, his arms folded, gripping a cigarette, his pop-eyed stare fixed on Smith's approach.

Smith strode past the entrance, pushed between the hedges and stepped to the knee-high brick wall surrounding the rose garden as he had seen neighbors do, placing himself below the gargoyle's window.

"What's going on, Mr. Dezmun?"

Shocked by Smith's directness, the janitor tossed the cigarette and waved his hands frantically, close to his chest, imploring Smith to stop acting so overtly.

"No," Smith protested. "Up until now, you've been the one choosing the spots and moments for our meetings. Well, I'm calling a meeting right here, right now. And we're going to use complete sentences. No more pantomimes."

Dezmun grimaced. His expression showed none of the presumption or pleasure of the earlier encounters; it was disapproving, as if Smith had pursued his task in all the wrong ways. He peeked up at the neighboring windows facing the street, which were dark and vacant or were illumined with the shades pulled down. Then he glanced behind him into his gloomy apartment.

Smith lowered his voice. He spoke more slowly, thinking that Dezmun would have trouble understanding him. "I went to the police."

Dezmun clutched his hair and mouthed a word: *No*.

"Yes. Police. I went. They did nothing. They pretended to be concerned at first but did all they could to keep me away from the facts." He doubted that Dezmun understood but continued nevertheless. "They assaulted me, physically and mentally, but that's another matter. Afterward, I went to Chinatown. I thought I had a contact but that fizzled. Or else I left too soon. I waited more than an hour, and still I may have left too soon. I want to go back there, and I suggest you tell me specifically where I should go. I suggest you write it down, legibly so that I can understand it. Or have your wife write it down or your son or nephew or somebody. And give me people's names. Real names, from the real world. No more mythology."

Dezmun's glance had stopped flitting, and his hands hung limply over the ledge. The censure was gone from his demeanor, and a muted gleam had returned to his eyes, not the familiar salaciousness, but pity and resignation, as if he recognized both Smith's plight and his own inability to direct Smith any further.

He adjusted his glasses, leaned out the window and extended his right arm down toward Smith who was still beyond his reach. Dezmun's hand opened and closed, as if hoping Smith would grasp it.

From Smith's memory sprang that inflexible image: the statue in the park. The Iron Men. The shipwrecked sailors. One kneeling, one standing and shouting, and the third, whom Dezmun now modeled, reaching down, over the gunwale, to pull the fourth, the drowning man, on board.

Smith noted his own resemblance, too, and asked himself, were he caught in the water, gasping to keep his head above the waves, would he not grab the offer of assistance, the chance to save himself from perishing, even while the boat itself was going down?

He started to reach for the gargoyle's hand.

Abruptly a figure lunged up behind Dezmun and pulled him inside. The bulky Lupo now filled the opening.

"Get your sick ass out of here!" raged the piggish face.

Smith stood his ground. "I demand to speak with Kogat Dezmun."

"I said get lost, scumbag! You don't belong here."

"Wrong! I . . ."

"You belong in prison, you pervert. I told you, leave that man alone. He's sick, and you're making things worse. You're making things worse for everybody."

"I don't believe you."

"Fuck you! You're lucky I don't come out there right now and bash your face in, you wise-guy piece of crap!"

A shouting match ensued: Lupo spouting profanity, Smith insisting on the justness of his inquiry and the malevolence of his enemies, among whom he now accused Lupo of being the ringleader. The argument ended when Lupo slammed the window shut, leaving Smith alone but triumphant for having succeeded, at least for the moment, in chasing the gargoyles away from their post.

He looked up at the windows and, as he did so, a half dozen of his neighbors, attracted by the uproar, immediately withdrew. But he knew that they were listening. Like a master of ceremonies addressing an audience, he extended his arms upward. "So you like watching a man drown!" he shouted. "Well, the show's over, ladies and gentlemen! Go back to your television sets! I'm not going under!"

FIFTEEN

Once upstairs, after showering and putting on dry clothes, Smith paced through his apartment, noting, as if for the first time, the emptiness of the rooms. The white walls, freshly painted, had no pictures, no posters, no calendars, no hangings of any kind. On the desk sat his guidebook, his notepad, his pens, maps, cookbook, dictionary, the book about sports, the telephone books, the biography of the actress Gloria Stevens, but there were no other bookshelves or cupboards or display cabinets or end tables in the room. Just the floor lamp, the sofa, the television. No knickknacks, no curios, no stray items, no houseplants; not a hat or a glove or a jacket; no letters, no paper clips, no rubber bands. Throughout the apartment there was no indication that anyone but he had ever lived there. None of his sister's personal belongings were available. The bathroom medicine cabinet contained only his toothbrush, his tube of toothpaste, his razor, his shaving cream. The kitchen cabinets were bare: not a dish, not a glass, not a coffee cup. A single ceramic cooking pot sat on one of the stove burners. Inside the refrigerator he found only the carton of eggs and the orange juice he had purchased on moving day. In the bedroom, he searched the closets and the dresser drawers, found nothing, shifted the bed, turned the mattress, stretched his hand behind the radiator, moved the chest of drawers away from the wall, hunting for a sock or a hairpin or some other personal item that had fallen back there, but here, too, he discovered just an undisturbed layer of dust.

He went into the living room and sat down on the sofa, his head spinning as if he were drunk. He envisioned repeatedly Walter and Bones scrambling up and over the fence. He should have waited longer, he realized; the pair might have reappeared moments after he left.

He sprang up and marched into the kitchen to peer out the window. The gargoyle window was still closed and unoccupied. Carin's husband, Edgar, had just stepped outside and was lighting a cigarette. He tossed the match and headed up the street.

He had probably just finished dinner, Smith reasoned. Though night had fallen, children on the street continued playing; perhaps Carin's children were also outside.

He put on his shoes and went down the hall to apartment 4F.

"Who is it?" the soft voice called seconds after he rang the bell.

"It's your neighbor from 4B."

The peephole clicked. He smiled at the invisible eye. Then the locks snapped open, and Carin's guarded face peered from the opening, behind the security chain.

"Good evening, Carin. Sorry to disturb you. I was wondering if I could ask you a few more questions concerning something we discussed the other day. If you recall, at the end of our last chat, we agreed to continue the conversation at some point in the near future."

"No, we did not agree."

"Yes, we did. I suggested that we meet again to share tips on job hunting. Remember?"

"I don't think I can help you more with job hunting. I said to you everything I know."

"Actually, I wanted to talk to you about something else."

"I don't think I can today."

"Please, Carin, if I could talk to you for just a few moments. I've been having a bit of a problem regarding something, and you may be able to help me. I'd rather not discuss it in the hallway. Please, Carin. Just for a few minutes. I really need your help."

Carin seemed caught between her vigilance and her need to be neighborly. She compressed her lips, hesitated just a moment before closing the door, unlatching the chain and reopening her apartment for Smith to come inside.

She wore a white blouse with red polka dots, black slacks and house slippers. As he followed her into the kitchen, he peered down the hallway and glimpsed, in the corner of a rear bedroom, two blank walls and a wooden floor. The kitchen, which four days earlier had flaunted window plants, teacups and placemats, was today unadorned, the chinaware and bric-a-brac packed in cardboard boxes stacked in a corner against the refrigerator.

"The painter is coming," Carin explained.

Smith surveyed the packed boxes and cleared counters. "I am sorry I cannot offer you tea or coffee."

They sat down at the table.

"I have to leave soon to pick up my children."

"Good. Then we have some time."

Carin's hands lay palms down and perfectly still on the tabletop.

"How was your job interview?" Smith asked.

She tilted her head and brought her brows together, appearing puzzled.

"The other day you said you were going to have a job interview."

"Oh, yes," she remembered. "It was good."

"Did you get the job?"

"I don't know yet."

Her eyes moved nervously to the window, to the floor, to her hands, which lay there uselessly with no china to fondle.

"How did you find it?" Smith asked. "Did you look in the newspaper?"

"Yes, I looked in the newspaper."

She frowned, folded her hands, interlocking her long fingers. The healthy nails gleamed with a pink transparency.

"I have an interview tomorrow," he said. "For a job in industrial design."

"Yes. I remember."

He knew that he had not mentioned his profession to her. She was confused, or else she was lying.

"This afternoon I went to Chinatown."

"Chinatown is very interesting," she said, unclasping her hands, laying them on the table.

"By the way, have you ever heard of someone called the one true beggar?"

"No." She placed her hands in her lap and looked out the window.

Smith stayed focused. "I may have had a dream about him, about the one true beggar."

Carin's green eyes, which on this second visit had squinted only out of puzzlement, fixed on Smith imploringly.

"I think I've seen him somewhere before," he said.

"It could be somebody you knew in the past, when you were a boy."

"No, I've seen him recently, perhaps on the day I arrived."

"I have this same feeling sometimes," she said.

"The same feeling? Is it possible for two different people with completely separate nervous systems to have the same exact feeling?"

Carin put her hands together and started kneading them. "Please," she said. "You wanted to ask me some questions. I must go soon, to pick up my children."

"Yes, of course, to pick up your children. By the way, I haven't told you yet that in my opinion you speak excellent English."

"Thank you." For the first time in his presence that evening she smiled. "I came here when I was a teenager."

"Everyone is from somewhere else, it seems."

She agreed. "But once we are here, we do not feel lost."

"You know, I've heard that before, or something to that effect. More than once. 'No one ever gets lost. Everything is under control. Everybody gets what he deserves.' How did it go? 'Render to every man his due.' I don't accept that anymore. Too much appears out of place. Or maybe something is in place at one moment and out of place the next. Take me, for instance: Am I where I should be right now, here, in your kitchen, talking to you? Or should I be trapped inside a box? That boy, for instance, the one we talked about last time, was he in his proper place? How can anyone confined in a box be in his proper place? How can he even fit in such a small space?"

"Oh, dear!" Carin pressed her fingers to her lips.

"I was wondering if you've heard anything new about this case. Maybe you saw something on the news or read about it in the newspaper."

"I do not know anything about this horrible story except what you say to me."

She started running her fingertips along the edge of the table.

"On Monday, you told me that you did hear about this case or a case just like it," Smith said. "Think for a moment. We see so many notices during the day. You might have heard something, which now you don't remember. Sort of like my dream."

She balled her hands into fists of frustration. "Why do you talk and talk about this terrible story?"

"Why do I need to justify being concerned for a missing boy who may still be alive?"

Carin winced.

"He may be languishing inside a wooden box, suffocating, terrified, desperate for something to eat or just for a hand to reach between the slats and stroke him on the cheek."

Carin looked at the window, then at the floor.

"He may be totally isolated and far removed from even the fuzziest memory of gentleness."

Her eyes welled with tears.

"He may be naked," Smith went on. "He may die naked."

She said nothing.

"Of course, that Sanderson boy and the one in the box may in fact be two different boys. And there was also the one I saw described on the poster in the window of the bagel shop. I can't remember that child's name. There are probably other missing boys. There has to be at least one missing boy. No one can disprove that."

Her hands lay on the table like dying flowers. To him, she was no longer pretty. The conspicuous veins in her temples rendered her complexion cold and pallid. The only color was in the rosy edges of her nostrils. Even the crooked tooth was now just a defect.

"Do you worry about your children?" he asked.

Her eyes snapped up, shocked and fierce. "Of course I worry about my children."

"Where are they now?" he asked.

"These are my children you are talking about," she hissed. She stood up with her back to the sink.

"I'm sorry, Carin. It's just that I don't want to dream one night about one of your cute little children being kidnapped, locked in a box and offered for sale in some alleyway in Chinatown."

She covered her ears, shut her eyes and ducked as if a bomb had exploded.

"How can you be certain, for example, that your son, your little alabaster boy, is exactly where you think he is at this very moment?"

"Stop it!" Carin screamed. "Stop it!" She lowered her hands. "How can you imagine such horrible things?" She tried to regain her composure but was breathing too hard. "It is time that you go," she announced. "Leave my home." She wrapped her arms across her chest and clenched her lips.

Smith stood up but stayed on his side of the table. "This whole affair has had a depressing effect on me," he said. "I've changed. I can feel that. I just wanted to get settled. I tried my best to be polite and do what was right. But when I hold an elevator door open for an elderly gentleman, he turns his back on me. I ask an otherwise friendly waitress to accompany me to Chinatown, and I'm treated like an armed robber and chased out of the establishment. I relate the rumor of a crime to the police, and I get cross-examined as if I were the kidnapper, as if I were the one stealing young boys."

Carin's face receded into doubt and disbelief before surging to a stronger panic. "Go now!" she demanded, but her voice was weak. Her hands trembled. "My husband will be back soon."

Smith ignored her. "All this talking has made me cynical. I turn people into metaphors: An old woman with large round sunglasses takes on the head of a fly; an old man inching along with a cane is a crab dragging a broken leg; fat men become elephants; the homeless are wild, starving dogs nosing around for food. And right now I'm sitting here watching you turn into a skeleton. But the boy is not just an imaginary flourish, or is he? Until I know for sure, I have no choice but to believe. Otherwise, I'd have to take a long look at myself in the mirror and admit, once and for all, that I am not the person I thought I was."

She darted away from the sink, attempting to reach the foyer, but Smith blocked her advance. She staggered back up against the sink.

In his mind, her thin figure divided the room: fluorescence by the window, shadow by the refrigerator. Smith raised his hand and held it vertically with the fingers straight, the palm flat, edgewise, lined up and down the center of Carin's frightened face. He peeked around the back side of his hand, at the left side of her face, then looked past the palm, at her right side. "Two halves," he announced. "Two faces. Where's the whole Carin? Is she there? I'd like to meet her."

"Please," she murmured. Tears had broken free and were coursing down her cheeks.

Smith stepped toward her and touched her lips with his fingertips. She snapped her head aside as if careening from a slap. He took her hands. She yanked them away and held them, balled and trembling, under her chin. He touched her temple, tracing the curve of the prominent vein. She closed her eyes. More tears rolled down. "Please go," she pleaded breathlessly. Her two fists offered stiffened resistance.

"You did invite me here," he reminded her.

His touch made her shiver, like the scrape of a knife. She gasped and bit her lower lip.

Smith pulled back, disappointed, having obtained nothing: no clues, no evidence, no information whatsoever, not even a cup of tea.

He left the kitchen and went to the door where he had trouble with the locks, turning them one way, then the other, finally getting them open and stepping out into the hallway. Carin watched from the kitchen until the door started to close, at which point she scrambled after it and, as it slammed, secured the doorknob, bolted the locks, latched the security chain.

"I'm tired of talking in empty rooms!" he shouted at the unresponsive door. "And I'm tired of being misunderstood! What is it that you're thinking? That's what I want to know!"

He felt the stillness of the hallway and the presences lurking behind each door. He half-expected a neighbor to appear, in which case he would walk by the person without acknowledging him in any way. Small talk led to a dead end, and the only thoughts he trusted were his own.

SIXTEEN

The ringing phone jerked Smith out of an empty sleep. The night before, he had collapsed on the bed without having drawn the shades, and the rising sun now blinded him.

He hoped it was his sister.

"Hello? Mr. Smith? This is Detective Brinkman from the 114th precinct. How are you this morning?"

"I'm fine."

"Glad to hear it. I'm just calling to let you know they found the Sanderson kid a couple of days ago."

"A couple of days ago?"

"He's just been identified. I don't know the details. Zimmerman has to file a report."

"Is the boy alive?"

"I'm afraid not."

"May I read the report once it's filed?"

"I'm afraid not. It's confidential. There's not much more I can tell you."

"Are you sure it was the Sanderson boy?" Smith asked.

"Positive."

"Was he in a box?"

"There was no box."

"Was he naked?"

"Look." The voice grew taut. "I just called to let you know that the case you were concerned about is closed. You should thank me for taking the time."

Brinkman hung up, and Smith's first thought was of how tired he was feeling.

It was Thursday. Interview day.

For breakfast, he boiled an egg, which cracked in the pot, spilling yoke like flaxen blood. As he waited for the egg to cook, he watched the sun slide into the kitchen on an unfamiliar angle, shaping in the corner a pyramid of daylight.

After breakfast, he opened the yellow pages and thumbed through the ads for lawyers: divorce and custody lawyers, bankruptcy lawyers, real estate lawyers, malpractice lawyers. One of the ads read: "Harris and Bulb. Experienced Defense Attorneys. White Collar Crime. Drug Arrests. Homicide. Weapons Possession. DWI. Sex Offenses. Free Consultation. 24 Hour Emergency Service."

Nothing about wooden boxes or stolen boys.

A lawyer was a bad idea anyway, he concluded. Nor would he talk to newspapers or television. No more begging, he decided; no more bargaining. This was a problem he would solve on his own. And he had to avoid confrontations and stop making scenes; he needed to become more discreet.

He opened up the street map to pinpoint the location of the Conrad Building where the interview would take place, but instead of laying the map flat on the desk and finding the corresponding quadrant, he folded it back up and repeated the actions accordion-style, unfolding it, refolding it, twisting it at first but soon with practice managing it smoothly and skillfully before closing it a final time and putting it aside. Next, he sat at the desk for some last-minute priming, but rather than write questions and answers, he doodled, tracing double-bows, helixes, spirals and curlicues.

Nothing intelligible or pertinent occurred to him. Nothing but boxes and boys.

He had an idea. Inside the recycling closet by the stairwell at the end of the hallway lay discarded newspapers, from which he salvaged the Monday and Tuesday editions mostly intact and sections of Sunday and Wednesday and brought them to the desk in his living room. He then systematically searched the recycling closets on other floors, tiptoeing guiltily up and down the stairs, mindful that his scavenging trespassed on the janitor's domain. Between the third and second floors he encountered a man with long sideburns and a leather jacket coming out of an apartment. Neither spoke, and the moment passed easily in cool and mutual indifference. By the time Smith returned to 4B, he had assembled nearly complete editions for the previous five days, and for the next hour he pored over the papers, skimming the international and political news, the sports, the weather, scanning more closely the national and local pages. He read stories about fires, shootings, corporate mergers, rapes, murders, tax evasions. Under "News Briefs" headlines read: "Woman Dropped Baby Out Window, Police Say"; "Bronx Man Shoots 3 Before Killing Himself"; "New York State Considers Changing License Plates." Halfway through a Tuesday section, just as he was about to take a break from the tedium, he spotted, at the bottom of a column reporting the outbreak of food poisoning, a terse article, a filler totaling six lines. The headline announced: "Body of Child Found." It was dated August 20 and stated:

The body of an unidentified male child was found this morning on a Hudson River pier near Perry Street. The body was discovered at six a.m. by a jogger. Cause and approximate time of death have not yet been determined. According to a police spokesperson, no eyewitnesses have come forward.

He tore out the article, folded it, then slipped it inside his wallet. Next he opened up the city map, this time laid it flat, located Perry Street in the index, found and examined the quadrant shaped by the coordinates, which contained the edge of the island, a yellow highway, the blue of a river, and two tiny white bars representing piers.

He would visit the scene after his interview, for which he now got dressed, putting on for the first time his light blue shirt, silver tie and gray suit. He felt adroit and pre-pared, especially once he took hold of the portfolio con-taining his design work.

Outside, the weather had been transformed. The thun-derstorms had washed away the summer. The air was dry and almost cool, the sky crystal cerulean, without a cloud or a wisp of haze. The sun embraced him with a tran-quilizing warmth.

Then he surprised himself: He stopped, turned, waved vigorously to the gargoyle and said "Good morning" loud enough for any neighbor to hear. He had not ex-pected to turn and wave and certainly not to say hello, and even more startling for him was the response of Mrs. Dezmun, who raised one of her sandstone forearms and countered his salutation with a languid flapping of her hand.

SEVENTEEN

Fifty-fifth Street was filled with the invariable fumes and clamor of double-parked trucks, handcarts, bicycle messengers, a maintenance crew. This time Smith did not stand still like a stone in the stream but joined the flow, barely glancing at the boutiques and the jewelry shops as he raced along, halting once to check the address on the business card he carried.

He found the glass doors of the Conrad Building and entered a lobby of granite floors and black marble walls, with potted palms and matching sculptures of muscular torsos whose heads and arms were broken off.

In the directory he located the Berenson Corporation: Suite 1509.

A stiff and silent crowd rode with him in the elevator. Everyone looked up or down, and no one said a word. Smith got off at fifteen and started down the corridor in the wrong direction but soon retraced his steps and found the suite. There was no buzzer, so he opened the door and walked in.

An elderly man was waiting in the antechamber. Behind the reception desk a woman with long red nails and a nasal voice was on the telephone.

"He hasn't called back yet, has he?" she was asking while rearranging memo pads. "He said he'd call back, and where is he? Hold on a minute." She looked up. "May I help you?"

"My name is Smith. I have an appointment with Dr. Weber."

"Please have a seat."

She was very much the kind of receptionist he had imagined during his visualization exercises, and the antechamber was similar to what he had predicted. The resemblances helped put him at ease. There were leather chairs, an end table with a lamp, a maroon carpet, paneled walls and two abstract paintings, each showing overlapping blue rectangles against a white background with the rectangles arrayed as if they were marching in staggered file.

Smith sat down on one of the chairs, across from the elderly man with sagging eyes and wispy hair. In his lap he held a russet cardboard file. The bulging seams were reinforced with masking tape, and around them he closed his nervous hands. Now and then he shook his head impatiently and clenched his jaw.

Smith leaned his portfolio crosswise against his knees, and, as if in response, the old man lay *his* file flat on his lap, then propped his elbows on the file and contemplated, with a frown, the empty spot on the wall above Smith's shoulder.

"Mr. Smith?" The receptionist turned away from the phone momentarily and pointed down a corridor that led to inner offices. "Office 7." She smiled. "Have a nice day."

The door was ajar, and Smith knocked softly before entering. The room, which was well lit through lucent panels in the ceiling, fit none of the layouts he had envisioned. Shades had been lowered over the windows, shutting off any view. The walls were undecorated. The floor had neither carpet nor parquet but vinyl tiles, beige and black squares arranged in a checkerboard pattern. Most surprisingly, there was no desk, neither rosewood nor mahogany. The office was small but not cramped; in fact, it was virtually unfurnished. There were shelves and a few books, a credenza with a pitcher of water and some glasses. There were no chairs, but, on the side opposite the shelves, next to the credenza, was a brown, tufted-leather sofa.

A man entered through an inner door, which he then closed behind him. Once shut, the door resembled a closet, and Smith would not have guessed that it opened onto a separate room.

The man was shorter than Smith, paunchy and wearing black slacks, tasseled loafers, and a dark brown, long-sleeve, turtleneck shirt. He was at least fifty, Smith guessed, and had blue eyes, red hair and a trimmed beard. When shaking hands, his grip was firm but damp and soft, like a child's.

"It's good to meet you, Dr. Weber."

"I'm not Dr. Weber. I'm Dr. Kennedy. Dr. Weber can't make it today, and so I'm here, among other reasons, to let you know that your interview has been rescheduled for tomorrow afternoon, same time, same place."

"Is Dr. Weber ill?"

"No, nothing like that. Please." He gestured toward the sofa. "Let's sit down."

They took the two ends of the three-person sofa, with Dr. Kennedy sitting nearer the credenza.

"Would you like a glass of water?" he asked, crossing his legs and settling in comfortably, sliding his arm along the back of the sofa and tapping his tasseled foot. He had been smiling continuously, but the smile was tight, constrained within the beard, more like a mischievous grin. The blue eyes, meanwhile, had a genuine gleam, conveying an elfin buoyancy.

Smith declined the offer of water. He leaned his portfolio against his side of the sofa and also crossed his legs to appear relaxed. He waited for the doctor to speak, but the doctor was waiting too, grinning.

"Are you a colleague of Dr. Weber?" Smith asked, breaking the ice.

"Indeed I am but not his substitute. As I said, this is not the interview. The interview is tomorrow afternoon, same time, same place. Dr. Weber will be here then to answer all your questions. What you and I are going to have today is a conversation; not quite a give-and-take, something more than chitchat, but by no means an interview."

"Chitchat can be quite challenging," Smith said, sounding positive.

"Oh, I hope our conversation doesn't degrade into chitchat." Kennedy hitched his shoulders as if holding in a laugh. His eyes sparkled at something unsaid, an amusing thought. For a moment, his foot rocked faster. "I'd like to offer you a glimpse behind the scenes, so to speak. May I ask you a few rather uninteresting questions first?"

"Certainly. That's why I'm here." Smith was eager to begin.

Kennedy rubbed his hands. "Let's start with an easy one: How have you been managing with this weather?"

"Awkwardly," Smith replied. "Either the air-conditioning is arctic or the heat is insufferable."

Kennedy seemed to admire the phraseology. "I hope in here it's neither arctic nor insufferable."

"No, I'm quite comfortable."

"Are you sure you wouldn't like a glass of water?"

"Yes, I am."

"Then let me ask you this: What foods have you been eating, for the most part?"

Smith was surprised by the question. "Eggs, mostly," he answered without faltering. "I tried roast chicken, but it didn't sit well."

"It seldom does."

"The mashed potatoes were watery."

"The consistency of oatmeal." Kennedy's shoulders again hitched up as he wrestled down a laugh. It seemed he would never release that clenched grin, so amused was he at the vague suspense that it caused. "Tell me,

Mr. Smith: When you eat, do you enjoy the tastes and textures of the food, or do you eat, for the most part, merely out of appetite?"

Smith laughed. What odd questions! The doctor's denials notwithstanding, he presumed that the interview had in fact begun. The strategy, it appeared, was for the interviewer to challenge the applicant with incongruous statements and questions and then assess the replies for intelligence, humor and verbal agility.

"I eat when I'm hungry," Smith answered. "Of course, the selections I make are either palatable or unpalatable, to greater or lesser degrees." He had meant the comment jocularly but saw the doctor nodding in earnest. "Thus far I've successfully managed my appetite."

"Have you read any good books lately?" Kennedy asked.

Smith drew a blank. The biography of the actress Gloria Stevens was all that came to mind.

"What about the telephone?" the doctor asked. "Do you know how that works?"

"Excuse me?"

"Do you know how a telephone works? You know what it looks like, you know how to use it, but do you know what makes it do what it does? Do you know how electricity works, how a television works? Can you explain why water flows out of a faucet when you turn it on?"

"I only arrived five days ago. That's not much time."

"Indeed."

Again, the doctor either missed the joke or did not find it funny.

"What about the people you pass on the street? Do you know what they're doing or where they're going, why they are where they are in the first place, what makes them tick, so to speak?"

"Up until now," Smith said, "the answers to these particular questions have not revealed themselves." His reply was weak. "But I'm sure I'll learn quickly."

"Learn quickly, indeed." Kennedy smiled and rubbed his baby hands. His dark outfit set off his shimmering eyes, and the restrained delight kept his grin clamped and glittering. He plucked at his beard, a nervous habit. "You know the look of things," he said, "the shape of things, the feel of things. But do you know what lies behind the things, inside the things, what inspires things? Do you understand the mechanism, so to speak?"

Here, Smith realized, was a man who liked to talk, who enjoyed the sound of his own voice, who probably recited poetry and sang songs when he was alone.

"Dr. Kennedy, I must say I'm becoming more and more puzzled by your questions. I don't mean to suggest that they're offensive, by no means, and I'll answer them as best I can, but they do strike me as highly irregular for a job interview."

"You assume, then, that this is a job interview."

"What else am I to assume?"

"Even though I told you three times—this makes four times—that we are not having an interview."

Smith shrugged. He was bothered by the cryptic talk and teasing tone. Still, he had to remain responsive and engaged. Almost from the start, he had lost the initiative and felt he could neither walk out nor let himself become angry. His getting the job could depend on how well he kept his composure.

He uncrossed his legs and sat up, grateful for the leather sofa though it was not exactly as he had imagined it, nor did the beige and black tiles fit his schemas. In addition, there were no window views, no office desk, no filing cabinets, and these he felt he needed.

"Do you enjoy talking to people?" Kennedy asked.

"Of course."

"Indeed! Do you find talking to people an easy thing to do?"

"That depends on whom I'm talking to. There have been difficult conversations." He liked the reply; it showed experience and was indubitably true.

"Do you have compassion for others?"

"I believe I do."

"Can you give an example?" Kennedy asked.

Finally the discussion appeared heading in a meaningful direction. Just as Smith had predicted, he was being asked to tell stories about himself.

Kennedy waited, grinning, picking at his beard.

"I always try to give the other person the benefit of the doubt," Smith said, hating the cliché as soon as it was uttered.

"The benefit of the doubt! How generous! Give me an example."

Smith was drawing a blank. What stupidity! He had foreseen this very juncture yet was woefully unprepared. Grabbing the first recollection that came to mind, he related the episode of the old man in the elevator—how he had tottered up the steps and almost lost his balance, how he had told Smith not to wait, how his hands had trembled, how he had rudely turned his back.

"What did you expect?" Kennedy asked.

Smith shrugged. "A little graciousness."

"Did you show graciousness?"

Smith was startled. "Yes. I believe I did."

"Did you introduce yourself, for example? Did you inquire into the man's well-being? Did you ask him how he was feeling? Did you invite him into your apartment or visit his apartment, ring his doorbell, ask him out for a cup of coffee? Did you even complain, politely and respectfully, let him know that you found his body language vexing, or at least ask him if anything was wrong? You said he walked with difficulty. Did you offer him help? Perhaps that elderly gentleman was perplexed by your just standing there without offering any assistance as he stumbled and nearly suffered a serious accident."

Smith laughed. "That's a bit of an exaggeration."

"That was how it may have felt to him for that frightening split second when he, as you put it, almost lost his balance."

Kennedy flashed his mischievous grin and clutched the muffled laugh. If given the opportunity, Smith thought, the doctor would answer his own oddball questions or play the sophist engaging himself in solo debates. For the time being, Smith decided to listen and demonstrate that he tolerated criticism and was prepared to learn from his colleagues.

"I don't mean to be rough on you," Kennedy said. "You may have simply focused on the wrong details. In any case, this confusion can never be prevented or avoided. Do you know why?" He smiled weirdly and prankishly.

"What confusion do you mean?"

"The confusion of never knowing on which details to base our understanding of things."

"I have to confess I have no idea," Smith responded cheerily. "What *is* the cause? Why all this confusion?"

"That was not the question, but the answer to each, I suppose, is the same: because of the dyad."

"Excuse me?"

"The dyad. The double helix. Truth and lies. The entwining strands." Kennedy wove his index fingers as they traced the abstraction in the air. "The genetic material, so to speak, of your social and moral understanding. Every assertion has a shadow strand, a denying double. It's always there, permanently operational." He leaned back and folded his soft hands on his paunch, assuming the pensive pose of having just imparted an axiomatic and totalizing fact.

Smith was merely bewildered. He knew his challenge was to sift nuggets of sense from an avalanche of nonsense or learn the secret code he was not grasping, all while remaining patient and amiable.

"Fact or falsehood," Kennedy continued, sitting up, plucking at his beard, tapping with his foot. "You don't know which. Even if confronted with irrefutable evidence, you still might not believe; you would still be free to believe otherwise. For example, I had told you three times that this *was not* the interview and still you believed that this *was* the interview. And now I'm telling you for the fifth time that this is not the interview, and still you are insisting to yourself that this could very well be the interview."

"Is it?"

Kennedy grinned, his eyes beamed. "It either is or it isn't. It can't be both. You see, the dyad is simultaneously stark and ambiguous: left, right; yes, no; black, white. Which is which? You don't know. The important point is that the Experiment isn't random. There is no accident. Everything fits perfectly. Nothing is left out. Every detail counts. Nothing is contingent. Nothing is subordinate. Everything is prescribed and managed, even the most fleeting, sidelong glances, even the briefest pause or equivocation."

He stopped. He could have said more, it seemed to Smith; he could have talked for hours. Instead, he yielded to the bottled-up chuckle and the teasing grin.

Smith *did* believe this was the interview and even now considered the possibility that Kennedy was Weber. As he had earlier suspected, the enigmatic presentation was designed to test his ability to think and react spontaneously. Thus far, he felt, he had made at best a neutral impression.

He tried another joke. "I suppose, if everything fits and nothing happens by accident, then there are no mistakes and every answer I give is correct. This is one interview I can't foul up."

Kennedy was amused. He held up his left palm, the five fingers spread, and the index finger of his right hand. "Six times," he intoned. "This is not an interview." He stressed each word. "Tomorrow. Same time. Same place."

Smith was silent.

"I'll tell you what." The doctor offered a concession. He leaned forward and lowered his voice conspiratorially. "If it will help you feel better, let's pretend that this *is* the actual interview. Of course, this *is not* the actual interview. This is merely a conversation. But between you and me, we'll make believe that this is the interview. Agreed?"

"Agreed." Smith hoped the silliness was over.

"So, tell me, Mr. Smith," Kennedy said, altering his voice to sound formal and mannered. With mock resolve he dropped his grin and furrowed his brow, put his cupped hands behind his head and gazed up searchingly as if drawing his questions out of the air: "How would you contribute to the firm?" Without waiting for an answer, he added: "Or how about this one: How do you find working with other people? Or furthermore: What leadership qualities do you possess? Let's try one more: Young man, how would you describe yourself? No need to give answers. I already know them all: Your name is Smith. You arrived five days ago from the West Coast, where you earned a master's degree in industrial design from a prestigious university. Currently, you're subletting your sister's apartment, 4B, at 30-30 36th Street, in Queens, New York. She's in Boston for the summer and is due back September 1, at which point you will move into your own place, always retaining the option of returning to the West Coast if, in the end, things do not work out as planned; an outcome, of course, largely to be determined by the results of the all-important interview, though naturally you don't intend to limit your contacts to only one firm. Have I left anything out?"

Dumbfounded, Smith slumped back. The leather sofa groaned beneath his weight. Inside him, a mirror cracked; there was a long fissure lengthwise down the middle of the glass, and neither fractured figure on either side was whole.

"How about that glass of water?" Kennedy asked. "Are you ready for it now?"

Smith refused, numbly shaking his head. He glanced at the pitcher and the glasses on the credenza. Rather than a glass of cold water, more than ever he would have liked a picture on the wall, a view out the window, a desk with a lamp and a parquet floor.

Kennedy giggled like an elf perched on stolen treasure. "You see! I really do know all the answers. Now this biography I've recited is extremely vague, and here exists an opportunity for you, assuming this were an actual interview, which it's not, to flesh out the character, so to speak. For instance, what's the name of that prestigious West Coast university that you attended?"

Smith made no reply.

"Which West Coast city did you come from?"

Smith did not answer.

"How about your sister?" Kennedy asked. "How old is she?"

He stayed silent.

"What's her name?"

He said nothing.

"Have you ever seen her? Can you conjure an image of her in your mind right now?" Kennedy waited.

As he listened, Smith viewed the puckish Kennedy in his varying lights: as a smirking pumpkin, loving the tease; as a brilliant scientist behaving like a naughty boy; as a mental patient whose handlers might barge in at any moment, apologize to Smith for the inconvenience and haul the gurgling Kennedy back to the asylum for a nap.

For the first time, Smith seriously considered standing up and walking out, but there remained one item he needed to hear discussed.

The pumpkin spoke: "You can't, can you? You can't tell me a single fact about this sister of yours. Indeed, you've never seen this unnamed sister. You've never spoken to her. Oh, yes. I'm mistaken. You have." He cleared his throat, and then, in a high-pitched, girlish voice, recited: "Hi! I'm not home now, but I'd love to talk to you, so leave your name and number, and I'll get back to you as soon as I can. See ya!" He made the high-toned beep and then, putting his hand to his ear as if holding a telephone, in a deeper, dumb-sounding monotone announced: "Hi, it's me, uh, I arrived today, uh, all's gone well, uh, I'll try to reach you again soon, uh, unless I hear from you first, uh, bye, uh." A hissing laugh issued through the frozen grin. "There it is," he proclaimed jauntily. "That's it. There's your sister. There's her brother. No more, no less. What a pair!"

Into Smith's startled consciousness flashed the memory of nighttime hammering and Lupo handling an electric drill. Had eavesdropping devices been installed next door to him? Were his phone calls being recorded?

Kennedy, who had slumped down, uncrossed his legs and pulled himself up. "Let's try something closer to home," he suggested. "What's your name? Your real name? Do you have a real name? 'Smith' sounds to me like a made-up name."

"Smith is my real name."

"When were you born? When's your birthday?"

"Do you want to know my sign?"

Bursting forth from a tossed-back head, after so much struggle and so much restraint, the doctor's glee finally erupted: For a split second the mouth gaped cavernously inside the beard, and laughter roared from a trembling gut. "This is fun!" he exclaimed, catching his breath. "More than I had expected."

"Perhaps we should get back to the interview," Smith feebly proposed, struggling to restore at least a semblance of control. "Pretend or otherwise."

"Or otherwise. Yes, of course, except that there is no otherwise."

Even a pretend interview, Smith decided, was preferable to the doctor's deeper foolishness. He took the lead: "I'm seeking a position in product design."

"Fascinating field!"

"I believe I am a creative individual who knows . . ."

"Who knows how to use fresh ideas, et cetera, et cetera." Kennedy resumed the mocking tone. "Young man, have you had any real-life experience in the field of product design?"

"Yes, I have."

"Indeed!" He showed fake surprise. "Such as?"

"I have in my portfolio several fully formed ideas."

"Fully formed ideas! My, my! How intriguing! Can you give me a for instance?"

"A dustpan."

"Now that's handy."

"I've developed a design that incorporates the concept of a rotational structure. Something like a revolving door."

"How ingenious!"

"I have the sketches here." He patted the portfolio at his side. "Would you like to examine them?"

"I would love to examine them," Kennedy confirmed. "Nothing would give me more joy. The problem is, they don't exist. Your portfolio is empty. There are no sketches, no fully formed ideas. Not even a stale, half-baked idea. You know nothing about design. You have a few clichés rattling around in your head. That's all. When you get home later, take a look inside that portfolio and see for yourself. Don't look now. It would be too embarrassing."

Smith was tempted to grab the portfolio and open it to prove he was who he claimed to be, but he imagined the doctor roaring derisively at his taking the absurd charge seriously and feeling compelled to refute it. "Why would I come to an interview with an empty portfolio?" he asked as calmly as he could.

"Odd behavior, isn't it? Then again, this is not the interview." Kennedy held up one hand and four fingers of the other, indicating the number nine.

"I give up," Smith said with finality. "What's going on? What are you up to?"

"Good questions. What's going on?" Kennedy waved his hands to take in the entire room and everything beyond it. "The Experiment. What am I up to? The Experiment. At least that's what I like to call it. You can call it something else. You can call it anything you want. Any word we use is accurate in some narrow sense but at the same time is totally imprecise. Tell me: When you walk on the streets, through the crowds, what does it feel like? What's your impression?"

"Like I've stumbled into a beehive."

"Good answer. Millions of bees, busy or just wasting time buzzing in a circle. What if I were to tell you, though, that all those busy bee-people were technicians, so to speak, in what I'm calling—again, for lack of a more exact term—the Experiment? What if I were to say that the receptionist outside this office was a technician? The men and women in the elevator, the panhandlers asking for money on the street: all technicians, each alone, each in concert, constructing the grand and all-encompassing concoction. Now there's a possibly viable label: The Concoction." After considering it, he shook it off. "No. I'll stick with 'Experiment'. And of course, I need not mention that you are included. In fact, you're the subject and single focal point of the whole contrived shebang."

Smith gazed uncomprehendingly while Kennedy glowed with the assurance that all he had elaborated made perfect sense.

"Now let me remind you," he said, growing serious, "I base the terms 'technician' and 'experiment' not on dictionary definitions but on metaphor. Strictly speaking, there are no white-coated lab technicians. Nevertheless, there exist parameters structuring and constraining this enterprise and, by extension, your experience and, by further extension, exactly who you are and what you will become."

Smith interrupted, inspired by a clarifying question: "Are you, by any chance, mistaking me for somebody else?"

The doctor tossed his head back and out bellowed another belly laugh, which filled the vacuum like a burst of exploding gas. "I know you're not joking," he whimpered, gripped by quaking mirth. "But it's hilarious just the same. No, sir, Mr. Smith: I am not mistaking you for somebody else. I don't believe I could."

"Then make your metaphors less opaque."

"Less opaque." Kennedy contemplated the request, playing with his beard. He crossed his legs and started tapping. "Imagine we have before us a script for a play. I am the playwright and director. You are the lead actor, except you don't know the text. You've never seen it. You recognize the set, but you have no idea what to say or what movements to make. Despite all this, you recite your part perfectly. No miscues. Your co-actors know the scenes precisely. They've read the script in its entirety.

You see, the surrounding phenomena you regard as short-lived and spontaneous have already been determined and rehearsed. The individuals you speak to, pass on the streets, overhear in conversation are there because they have been placed there by the playwright and director. As stated earlier, nothing is accidental. There are no monadic events. Each is interconnected and constitutes the whole, leaving us with a terribly complicated piece of machinery."

Smith was impatient with the analogy, which seemed irritatingly absurd and juvenile. "Let me see if I understand you correctly," he ventured. "Are you suggesting that the man in the elevator I told you about earlier . . ."

"Technician."

"And the guy on the subway, the one who smelled like salami, and Wendy the waitress, and even the elderly gentleman sitting in the waiting area right outside this office?"

"Technician, technician, technician." Kennedy pointed at each enunciation. "And coincidence? Two events occurring simultaneously for no apparent reason? Randomly, as it were? Well, trust me: There is no such thing."

"So what you're suggesting is, now that I'm up here with you, down below there's nothing going on, and if I were to walk to the window and raise the shades and look outside, I would find an empty street."

Kennedy smiled, enjoying the challenge. "Try us," he said, almost tauntingly. "Go ahead. Give it your best shot. Go to the window and take a peek. Try to catch us napping. You see, even if you did take what you felt to be a sudden, unplanned, unexpected, unrehearsed peek, that, too, would be part of the Experiment."

Smith stayed put, determined not to play the fool. "This is quite a conspiracy you're describing."

Kennedy winced. "No, not a conspiracy. Choose another metaphor, but please don't say conspiracy; even if, like all the others, the word contains its grain of accuracy, it sounds too criminal and sinister. Believe me, Mr. Smith: We are benign." He smiled reassuringly. "You have no choice, of course. There's nothing else. Nothing beyond. Nothing outside. Just you and the Experiment or whatever we decide to call it. That's it. Nothing but. Case closed."

Case closed. Smith had heard that phrase before.

"So that makes me a nobody," he concluded, smirking doubtfully while hiding a deeper fear.

Kennedy shrugged and showed his hands, as if no other inference were possible. "I'm open to suggestions," he said. "I'm willing to entertain a fully formed idea, but I've yet to hear one."

Smith said nothing.

"Who are you, Mr. Smith? Are you somebody, or are you nobody? Are you a complete package, with a conscience, a will, an emotional inventory, a personality, a history? If so, tell me about it. I'd like to hear."

More clearly now, Smith saw the man was insane.

Kennedy piddled with his beard, rocked with his foot, and his eyes kept giggling with confidence and waggishness; they seemed impossible to surprise. "Tell me, Mr.

Smith: Do you know of anything that happened before you arrived in New York?"

Smith had endured enough. He determined the time had come to walk out, but still he remained seated; the sofa was so comfortable, and he had not yet said all he had to say.

"Do you know of anything at all beyond the range of your circumscribed experience?"

Smith was annoyed. "What are you suggesting? That everything is fake?"

"Oh, no. To me, it is all very real: this sofa, this office, me, you, the future. Your future, in fact, is so real I've actually examined it, practically held it in my hands, so to speak. It's all already there. Within the parameters, of course."

"Inside, yes. Outside, no," Smith muttered to himself.

Kennedy overheard. "Exactly! You see, you may have imagined the presence of free-willing entities and multiple points of view, but in actuality there are only two perspectives: yours and mine—'mine' meaning the Experiment's—and upon the second, the first is completely contingent. Of course, an individual cannot pursue divergent futures, so while you may possess particular desires and appear to make particular choices, I already know what they are. I've already made them for you." He gestured with his infant hands toward everything around him. "That is, this wild conglomeration has." The word impressed him. "I like that. Conglomeration. A bit of a mouthful, though." He shook it off. "Let's stick with 'Experiment'."

The doctor held his pose—amused, observant, keenly intelligent, thoroughly ridiculous.

Smith thought that if this man's presentation was an indication of how his firm conducted business, working for the Berenson Corporation seemed considerably less appealing than it had before the interview, or the charade, had begun.

Kennedy was giggling again. "I'm sorry, Mr. Smith. I suppose I shouldn't be teasing you like this, but what else can I do? I feel as if I'm watching an insect floundering in a jar: It bangs its head against the glass wall, thinking blindly that somehow it can bang through. You are so thoroughly transparent and predictable to a far greater extent than I had expected. Is there anything at all you can hide from me? Is there a single, solitary thought or fact that you possess that I do not?"

Smith reflected, surveying what he had learned, what he had experienced, combing his recoverable past for an incident or anecdote with which to confront the doctor's presumption. "You don't know how the egg I boiled this morning cracked in the pot, how the yoke oozed out and undulated in the water."

"Oh, but I do know," Kennedy retorted. "I do know how it undulated in the water."

"And if a strand of a woman's hair comes loose . . ."

"She swiftly and unself-consciously tucks it behind her ear."

"What about my dreams?" Smith blurted out. "You can't possibly know what they are."

Kennedy dismissed the objection by wiggling his stubby fingers. "Don't confuse me with a psychiatrist," he said, "but why don't you describe for me the dream you had last night?"

Smith was silent.

"Go ahead. Tell me what you dreamed last night."

"I can't remember," he confessed.

Kennedy pounced: "For all you know you had no dream last night. For all you know, you've never dreamed."

That was not true. Smith remembered his first dream in New York, but this was not the moment to reveal it.

"Let's try this," Kennedy suggested. "Look in your wallet. One would think an ordinary person carried photos and identification in his wallet. Go ahead. Take a look."

"Another time."

"Take a look and see for yourself: no driver's license, no family pictures, no identification of any kind, no memories, no date of birth. Surely an authentic, fully formed, sharply defined individual would possess those items and could make them available upon request."

Smith made no move to comply. The dare was bogus, intended only to embarrass him. Besides, an authentic individual would not need to look in his wallet to see who he was; he would already know.

"Exactly what kind of doctor are you?" Smith ventured boldly. "Do you perform operations?"

"Metaphorically speaking. Or perhaps I'm more of a maintenance inspector. Now there's a comforting metaphor. I see to it that the mechanism functions. I fix loose parts, I tighten nuts and bolts, I oil creaking joints, I search out metal fatigue. In other words, I jiggle the details that make things flow. Or something like that."

Smith felt caught in a swamp of blather and pointlessness.

"Inevitably," Kennedy continued, "with such a sprawling mechanism, something snaps—a tiny rivet, a dried-out patch of glue. But that's not your concern. The overexcited mouse winds its way dutifully through the concocted maze. Just don't assume we never make mistakes. We do the best we can with the tools and materials at hand." He shrugged, arched his brow, admitting the obvious limitations.

"Poland and Brinkman," Smith suggested.

Kennedy threw up his hands in a gesture of concession. "The chain is as weak as its most incompetent links."

"Those links seem excessively rusted."

"They'll hold."

"And Kogat Dezmun? What's his role in this production? Mopping the hallways? Behaving like a lunatic?"

"It takes all kinds," Kennedy replied. "Even lunatics belong to the Experiment."

"Why is everyone trying to convince me that Kogat Dezmun is a lunatic?"

"You've met him. What do you think?"

"I think *he is* a lunatic."

"Well, then, who's trying to convince whom here?"

"Is Kogat Dezmun going to be liquidated?"

"Liquidated? Oh, my! You've been watching too much television. The man's sloppy. That's all. He's febrile and unreliable. That's all. He needs tightening. Nothing that a well-turned wrench can't repair. This is the Experiment, Mr. Smith, not the Mafia."

Smith was exasperated. "Why are you telling me this? Why expose the trick? Doesn't that spoil the fun? If the mouse knows about the maze, perceiving its design, as it were, it might just stop running."

"It won't. It will run even if it understands because it doesn't want to starve, and it will never be sure there isn't a way out. Actually, it's beneficial that you know. You will refuse to believe, but you will suspect; you will take second glances; you will interpret and reinterpret everything anyone ever says to you; you will question everything. Was that gesture spontaneous? Was that remark sincere? Was it genuine surprise on the stranger's face? Or did the person only pretend to be surprised? Was the compliment heartfelt or just a ruse to be polite? Did the eye wink signal an attraction, commence a seduction? Or was that but one more feature in the Kennedy amalgam? Should you have noted the other eye, the eye that stayed open, the cold, wary, critical, mediated, ungracious, unflattering eye?"

"The dyad," Smith said in a beaten-down tone.

"Exactly. Now that you know, you will never forget. You won't let go. You're trapped. This conversation will end. You will leave this office and have no idea what to think. Is the Experiment real and operational? How long will it continue? Even if you come to accept that it is real and operational, how will that understanding alter your outward behavior? I suspect not at all since you will never know for sure." Kennedy flashed his jeering smile. The bearded gnome had made his case, but Smith had something left to say, and the time had come to say it. His voice shriveled to a whisper, drying up and simmering on a final proposition: "What about the boy in the box?"

Kennedy's smirk vanished. His eyes went cold.

"Who is the boy in the box?" Smith asked. "Where is he?"

Kennedy moaned. "Don't start with that nonsense."

"The boy in the box?" Smith repeated. "What does that mean?"

Kennedy dropped back, as if displeased.

"Is there an actual boy in an actual box?" Smith asked. "A kidnapped boy? Maybe three, maybe four, maybe five years old? Is the box the kind they pack oranges in? What is it made of, plywood?"

Kennedy scratched his beard.

"Cheap pine? What? Tell me. What is it made of?"

The doctor placed his hands in his lap where they held each other meekly. His eyes revealed a tinge of sadness.

Smith chased the sudden advantage. "Is there a little boy imprisoned in a box somewhere? Is that what this is all about?"

Kennedy said nothing. He was grinning again, but the grin was forced. He looked tired. His shoulders slumped.

"Is this little boy naked, by any chance?"

Kennedy's eyes widened.

Smith laughed. "Why can't you answer these questions? Is that little boy the only thing you won't talk about?"

"You're being aggressive."

"Self-defense."

"Against what?"

"Your nonsense."

Both men smiled: a showdown of triumphant grins.

"So, what about it, Dr. Kennedy? Is there a boy in a box?"

"I'm disappointed. Up until this moment you've been a sensible young man. Practical and down-to-earth. Now you're dragging in this bogus fantasy."

"What about the Sanderson boy?" Smith asked. "Whose fantasy is *he*?"

"Trust me on this, Mr. Smith." The doctor spoke firmly, regaining control. "Each boy is exactly where he is supposed to be."

"I dreamed about the boy in the box."

"It wasn't your dream. It was a lunatic's dream. You, Mr. Smith, are not a lunatic."

He searched Kennedy's eyes for a motive or an insight but was thwarted by the shimmering regard. There were no chinks, no clues, no offers. Surrendering was all that remained. "Dr. Kennedy, I give up. You've played some game with me. I've tried to be a good sport. Sadly, you've told me nothing that, as far as I can judge, is worth knowing. Except, perhaps, that my interview has been postponed until tomorrow, and even that particular piece of information I find hard to believe."

"Oh, believe it, my friend."

"I don't see myself coming back."

"Please come back. Dr. Weber will be here tomorrow. I guarantee it." Kennedy leaned across the sofa toward Smith and lowered his voice to speak confidentially. "Between you and me, I'd say you have an excellent chance of getting the job. I'll definitely put in a good word. I've been impressed here today. You mustn't think otherwise. You've got spunk, contentiousness, a critical faculty. What's important is for you to leave here today understanding that the Experiment is operational despite occasional malfunctions. Just live your life and feel confident that, when you wake up in the morning, everything will be ready. Don't worry about the emptiness. We'll fill in the blanks."

"That seems to be the consensus: Don't worry, it's none of my business, everything is as it should be."

"Exactly!" Kennedy stood up. "Mr. Smith, thank you so much for coming. Enjoy the remainder of your day." He was pumping Smith's hand. "Have a nice dinner, a glass of wine. Listen to music. Be patient with the fallible heathen."

Smith wondered: Had he come through smashingly or failed utterly? Was the interview over, or had it not yet begun?

They drifted toward the door.

"Don't forget," Kennedy reminded him. "Tomorrow."

Then the two of them, speaking synchronously: "Same time! Same place!"

The doctor slapped Smith on the shoulder.

"May I have one of your business cards?" Smith asked dreamily.

"Sorry. I'm all out. I'll send you one as soon as the newest shipment comes in." Kennedy opened the office door. "By the way, you do resemble that actor. What's his name again?"

"Hamilton Baker."

"Yes!" Kennedy beamed. "You look just like Hamilton Baker!" He took Smith's elbow and guided him into the corridor.

"Is Dr. Weber a man or a woman?" Smith asked, hoping to come away with a single tangible fact.

"Let's leave that as a surprise."

"Will there be a desk?"

"Would you prefer a desk?"

"Yes, I would prefer a desk."

"The sofa didn't please you?"

"The sofa was wonderful. If anything, it was too comfortable, but I would still prefer a desk."

"I'll see what I can do."

With that, the neat beard, roguish eyes and gremlin smile slipped back inside the office, behind the closing door.

The receptionist was gone. The desk and the phones were dark. The antechamber was empty. Smith was alone. The blue rectangles were still marching on the wall, but the sleepy-eyed man with the expanding file had left the suite or else had entered one of the inner offices to be interviewed or conversed with or teased and tormented by his own malicious prankster.

Smith glanced back toward office 7 and contemplated returning, knocking on the door, opening it, stepping inside, reintroducing himself to whomever he found there, apologizing for being late, recommencing the interview, or the conversation, as if it had not already taken place. Surely, the second time, the ordeal would be much easier.

EIGHTEEN

"Perry Street," Smith told the driver. "Near the Hudson River."

As the taxi darted and crawled downtown, Smith winced at the memory of Kennedy's milky hand closing the inner door, of the arrogant trickster pulling a dyad out of his beard, of himself, the unprepared applicant, snared between a vague possibility and the cold, hard facts.

Was the boy in the box merely a lunatic's figure of speech? Five feeble syllables aimed at nothing real, planted in Smith's mind as a sick practical joke?

He checked himself. He would not give up. A dyad explained the ambivalent wink but could never disprove the boy in the box. He still had that first night's dream, which could not have been contrived or fixed within parameters other than his own. No one could register the windings of his unspoken thoughts; no one but he, and possibly not even he.

It was a sloppy operation, this Experiment: a flimsy gizmo, a lot of silly, unconvincing imagery about loose nuts and cracked bolts, descriptions that could entertain for half an hour or so in a semifurnished office, say, with lowered shades and a checkerboard floor, in an otherwise cramped and typical corner of a sprawling, incalculable world. He needed only to shake the scaffolding and the complete contraption would collapse.

The portfolio rested between his knees. Smith knew his creations were real, and if the sketches were missing from the portfolio, that could only be explained by his having forgotten to transfer them from one of his suitcases stored in the hall closet. He was not going to unzip the case now just to disconfirm what could never be. Such a gesture would accede to the Experiment, making him a willing participant, a conspirator against himself, a spy on his own soul. The mouse would know and still keep going, just as Kennedy had predicted.

The taxi left him on a leafy, residential street of red-brick homes and brownstones. The clarity of the sky and the sunshine ignited the pear trees so that the leaves gleamed with a vibrancy he had not seen before.

On the corner, the sparkling water of the river became visible, flowing parallel to a highway where cars whizzed by in both directions and above which the sky, released at last from the narrow streets, expanded brilliantly and cloudlessly, the sun bursting with a radiance that stabbed his eyes and made him cower as he waited for the traffic light to change. On the shoulder of the highway, joggers and dog walkers passed singly or in pairs. Not far off, a dilapidated pier extended into the water. The river shimmered, and on the opposite bank, low brown buildings crouched beneath the dazzling weight of the sky.

He crossed the highway, inhaling deeply, for the chill wind blowing in off the water tasted sweet in his nostrils and his lungs. He drew nearer the pier, which was sealed off by a chain-link fence topped by coils of razor wire. It stood on rotting piles and was concrete beneath a corroded layer of tar and spotty patches of brick. The surface glistened with broken glass, and between the bricks grew dandelions. At the edge of the pier, slabs of concrete had broken off and hung sloping toward the water, clinging tenuously, connected only by reinforcing rods and ready to be shaken loose in the next thunderstorm.

To the south rose the financial center, dominated by the two towers, which had acquired, in the clear air, viewed from a quiet distance outside the hive, the aura of abiding stillness.

He stopped a young man walking past.

"Excuse me. Do you know anything about the body of a boy that was found around here?"

"What was that?" The man had yellow hair and a ring through his eyebrow. He had been listening to headphones, which he now removed in order to hear.

"A boy might have been kidnapped, and his body might have been found on or near this pier. Do you know anything about that?"

"No, I'm sorry. I can't help you." The man slipped the headphones back on and hurried away.

Smith turned back to the pier, leaned his portfolio against the fence and spied through the chain link. Tied to one of the fence posts and stretching several feet along the tar was a yellow plastic strip. At the base of this post, by the concrete anchor, the lower part of the fence was detached. While crouching Smith could pull back the chain link, reach through and get hold of the plastic tape, pull it toward him and straighten it to read the black letters printed on it: "POLICE LINE DO NOT CROSS."

He studied the pier for further indications of a crime and spotted an object wedged between two bricks. He took off his jacket, got on his knees, widened the opening in the fence, reached his arm through up to the shoulder, pressing his face against the chain link, stretching with his fingertips just enough to touch the object and tip it into his palm. He withdrew his arm, dusted himself off and examined his find. It was a broken piece of wood—plywood, he believed—three inches long, two inches wide, jagged at one end, sawed off at the other; on one side was a line, faintly rose-colored, an inch thick, curved like the loop of a letter, an O, a G, a C or a D; or a number, a 9, a 6, an 8 or a 0. He scanned the ground for additional fragments, but any others had been swept away by the wind, carried off by trophy hunters or confiscated by police.

He put the piece of wood in the inside pocket of his jacket. Frail evidence, he had to admit: a newspaper clipping, a police cordon, a fragment of wood dislodged from a crevice between bricks on a disintegrating pier. A thorough search of any location might have kicked up equally suggestive material. The city was littered from end to end with trash and wood.

He considered tossing the wood over the fence and into the water, but it was just as easy to keep it in his pocket, and as long as he possessed it, he could further evaluate and perhaps reverse whatever conclusions he might draw. Regard the wood as telling proof or regard it as irrelevant debris: The choice would be arbitrary, and that single act of discretion torpedoed the Experiment, cutting him completely free.

He jogged back across the highway as the light was changing, turned down one of the shady side streets, with no particular destination in mind, and at the first corner came upon a cafe. There were tables in a patio area bordered by flower boxes. The dark interior was air-conditioned and eclectically furnished: upholstered arm-chairs, Formica-top tables, candlestick lamps. On the walls hung garishly colored paintings of jumbled body parts: arms, legs, torsos, fractured faces. The glass counter offered a bright display of cakes and pastries. Three of the four walls were exposed brick; the fourth was plain stucco and adorned not by lurid paintings but by a lone, stuffed iguana suspended from a hook in the middle of the sticky white desert.

Smith sat in a corner. Two other tables were occupied—one, across the room, by a pair of middle-aged couples engaged in lively conversation, the other, next to Smith's, by a young woman with brown hair, blue jeans and a tank top; a thin, pale, studious girl, wearing circular wire-frame glasses and reading a paperback book. When he sat down, she looked at him with a neutral glance, more alive but not completely unlike the stare of the stiffened iguana.

The waitress, in her early twenties, wore a black skirt, black fishnet stockings, an orange and black striped top; her lipstick was purple, her hair black with lavender streaks, her eyelids and her fingernails all painted black; the side of one nostril was pierced by a pearl pin, and a series of silver rings marked the outer length of her right ear. As far as he could see, the left ear had been left unencumbered.

"Want a menu?" she asked apathetically, her black eyelids hovering at the point of shutting.

Smith stared at the colors and the rings.

"Mister?"

"A cup of coffee," he said, "and scrambled eggs with toast."

"We don't have eggs."

"You don't have eggs?"

"Nope." She looked off to the side.

"How can you not have eggs?"

"What can I say? We don't have eggs." Clearly she did not care. "We have desserts. There's a fruit and cheese platter."

"I only eat eggs."

She shifted her stance and regarded him cautiously.

"Have a piece of cake," she suggested. "It's got eggs in it."

"Can I get the eggs without the cake?"

The waitress refused to smile but was bored, not annoyed. In the corner of his eye, Smith saw that the young woman with the round glasses had glanced at him as well.

"You look like a hornet," Smith remarked to the waitress. "The black and the orange. And the stockings are like bumblebee wings." He laughed at his description. "Translucent. I mean that as a compliment." He folded his hands under his chin. "We won't mention the stinger."

"Let me get you the menu."

"I'll just have a cup of coffee."

As he watched her netted legs retreat behind the counter, where she busied herself with his coffee, he wondered which of the details was the most revealing: the lattice or the flesh? Her boredom or her negligence? Her tedium or her gloominess?

The dyad beat the drum. And what else could he do but sit there like a customer waiting to be served?

When the waitress returned and set the cup of coffee down in front of him, he asked her, "Do you believe events transpire concurrently or sequentially by chance, as it were? Or do events, down to the most minute details, occur according to a plan? Or, if not charted by a plan consciously implemented by a controlling intelligence, then is each event linked and merged, involuntarily, as it were, and ineluctably, with all the others, the way bees mesh in a hive, say, or the way the net of your stockings meshes with your extremely sexy legs?"

She neither smiled nor frowned.

"What about the dyad? Do you know about the dyad?"

"A Chinese gang?"

Smith laughed. "The dyad bisects an idea, cuts it right in half, makes two statements out of one, reverses every thought." To illustrate, he pointed to his face, winked with his left eye, then his right. "See what I mean?" He winked his left eye: "Yes." He winked his right eye: "No." He winked left: "Telling the truth." He winked right: "Telling a lie. It's as basic as that. And I never know which is which, or even if there is a 'which is which', if there isn't a multitude."

"Mister," she sighed, "I've been awake since four o'clock this morning, and I have to work until midnight tonight, and to be perfectly honest, your conversation isn't making my life any easier."

"This is what I'm like when I don't get my eggs."

The waitress looked at the young woman and asked if she needed anything else.

"Just the check," the young woman said. Her voice was thin like a bird's.

The waitress walked away, and again the young woman glanced at Smith, this time maintaining eye contact for an instant before dropping her eyes in her book. She had been listening to him talk, Smith noted.

"Can you guess my sign?" he asked her.

The woman looked up, surprised at being addressed.

"My astrological sign," Smith explained.

"I don't really believe in astrology," she said.

"Neither do I. How about free will? I didn't have to walk in here, did I?"

"You can still walk out."

"Do I remind you of someone?"

At first the woman seemed bothered, then took a moment to study Smith's face. She had light blue eyes and a freckled complexion.

He gave her a clue: "A famous actor?"

"No idea," she stated blandly.

"Hamilton Baker."

She tilted her head to glimpse him from an altered angle. "I suppose." She was hardly enthusiastic. "I don't really like his movies."

"Actually, I haven't seen them myself."

She smiled weakly, tucked her hair behind her ears, then returned her attention to the paperback on the table. Smith allowed the silent pause to engulf her, and soon she was reading as intently as before he had walked in.

He wondered if she lived nearby, and, if so, whether she had been present when the missing boy had been found and had actually seen him. She might have collected the larger fragments of wood. He considered sliding over to her table and showing her the piece he had in his pocket. She might recognize it, become excited by it and be comforted. With his piece and whatever she had accumulated, the two of them, joining forces, could possibly reassemble major sections of the shattered box. How relieved he would be by such a confirmation: that an unscripted world thrived around him with time moving forward, that there were myriads of stars in the sky and a profusion of histories as complex as his own.

And who knew how many others were walking around with their undisclosed pieces of wood?

He caught himself from sprinting too far ahead of what he could reasonably expect. If he befriended this woman, he should not become overbold. Most of the individuals in whom he had thus far confided had sooner or later denounced him and become his enemies. Candid talk was a clumsy tool. When the moment was propitious, he would whip out the piece of wood and stake his claim to what was true. Until then, he would stay on the surface, stick with the familiar, with what was popularly desired, expected and appreciated. He reached into his jacket pocket and fingered his prize, just to reassure himself.

Casting aside his recollection of the humiliating interview, he decided to go back to the Conrad Building the following day, same time, same place. What did he have to lose? He was running out of money and needed a job. He would wear his suit and tie again, declaring his willingness to be seen as well as his right to be heard. It had been wrong to set so much store by the interview in the first place. A future would unfold whether or not he landed the job, whether it was Kennedy who greeted him or Weber or somebody else. There would be a desk, or no desk; it really did not matter after all. This time, the interviewer would make it easy for him. In the end, as they stood up, Smith would accept the congratulatory handshake that conveyed the coveted position.

He stopped daydreaming. For the first time, he questioned his talent and his fitness for his chosen profession.

He looked at the portfolio, which was leaning against his chair. Yes, he thought, it was possible that industrial design would turn out not to be his field. It could be he had no idea yet how best to participate in society. But he was armed with his wood, which fully compensated for the absence of designs, all of which would sooner or later have fallen into obsolescence anyway. It was a foolish philosophy, he realized, that tried to jam reality into a triangle just to scoop up dust.

Smith leaned toward the young woman reading the book. "Excuse me."

She lifted her head, displaying little surprise, as if she had expected the interruption.

"Have you ever seen the Iron Men?"

"Pardon me?"

"The Iron Men. A statue down in Battery Park."

"No, I don't believe so." She seemed curious. "What kind of a statue is it?"

"Well, basically, it shows four men during a shipwreck. It's hard to describe. Or, rather, it's easy to describe but impossible with words to convey the full effect."

"Are you an artist?" she asked, eyeing the portfolio.

"I haven't decided yet. What's your name?"

"Beth."

"My name's Smith, which I think I'm going to keep."

"Pardon me?"

"Well, I was thinking of changing my name to something less familiar, but now I'm not so sure."

She raised her brow skeptically.

"I suppose that's an odd thing to consider doing, but everyone must think about it once in a while. Beth is a nice name. By the way, Beth, do you like sculpture?"

"I love sculpture." Beth closed her book and laid her arms on top of it. "New York is great for sculpture." She leaned forward, arching her back. Her face had come alive.

"Well, I'm on my way to Chinatown," he said, "but first I'm going back to the park to take another look at that statue. If you're interested, you can join me."

He signaled to the waitress to bring him the check.

"It's possible," he told Beth, "that one of these sculpted figures was modeled after me. Or I was modeled after it. In any case, if you come with me, you'll be able to tell me which of the figures you think I most resemble."

Beth stared as if trying to size Smith up, to judge whether he was joking or being sincere, whether he was an interesting person or a disconnected soul.

"To tell you the truth," he said, "I don't think I look like any of them, but I'd like a second opinion. What do you say?"

Smith noted her puzzlement and indecision and in response bestowed upon her a pronounced wink, to which she replied with a spontaneous smile.

Finally, he had gotten a handle on things. He could not wait to call his sister and give her the good news.